ANGELA
and
DIABOLA

Also by Lynne Reid Banks

The Indian in the Cupboard
Return of the Indian
The Secret of the Indian
The Mystery of the Cupboard
The Key to the Indian

The Farthest-Away Mountain
The Fairy Rebel
I, Houdini

and for younger readers

The Adventures of King Midas
The Magic Hare
Harry the Poisonous Centipede

ANGELA
and
DIABOLA

LYNNE REID BANKS
ILLUSTRATED BY
KLAAS VERPLANCKE

Collins
An imprint of HarperCollinsPublishers

For Emily,
who knows a good book
when she hears one!

First published in Great Britain by Collins in 1977
Collins is an imprint of HarperCollins*Publishers* Ltd,
77-85 Fulham Palace Road, Hammersmith, London W6 8JB

The HarperCollins website address is
www.**fireandwater**.com

7 9 11 13 12 10 8 6

Text copyright © Lynne Reid Banks 1997
Illustrations copyright © Klaas Verplancke 1997

The author and illustrator assert their moral rights to be
identified as the author and illustrator of the work.

ISBN 0 00 675300 0

Printed and bound in Great Britain by
Omnia Books Limited, Glasgow

Contents

1. Birth

Mrs Cuthbertson-Jones was having a baby.

At least, that's what she had understood was happening.

She was lying in bed in a hospital with a big bump in her tummy and a nurse fussing around her, saying things like "It won't be long now!"

Mr Cuthbertson-Jones was not present.

"I'm sure you'll manage splendidly without me, dear," he had said, and vanished before she could mention the fact that lots of husbands stay with their wives when their babies are being born.

Mrs Cuthbertson-Jones thought he was probably in a pub somewhere, not even in a waiting room smoking heavily and pacing the floor, the way husbands do in movies. But she didn't mind.

She didn't mind that, or anything else, because she felt so extraordinarily happy and comfortable.

She was twenty-two years old and this was her first baby. She had heard that having a baby can hurt. But having this one wasn't hurting in the slightest. In fact she felt as if she were on a nice pink cloud somewhere up close to heaven.

The nurse thought she was being awfully brave. "I've never known anyone make less fuss," she said several times.

Mrs Cuthbertson-Jones was making so little fuss that after a while the nurse went out of the room for a cup of tea. While she was away, Mrs Cuthbertson-Jones suddenly decided that the nurse ought to come back right away. She pressed the bell she had been given. The nurse bustled back, looking a little annoyed because she had left her tea half-finished.

"I think the baby is coming now," said Mrs Cuthbertson-Jones pleasantly.

"Oh no, dear," said the nurse very firmly. "If it were, you'd know all about it!"

"I do know all about it," said Mrs Cuthbertson-Jones. "It's being born right this minute."

"Nonsense, dear," said the nurse. "You're not even pushing."

"I don't need to push," said Mrs Cuthbertson-Jones. "But it's coming just the same."

The nurse smiled in a superior way and was just about to say "Nonsense, dear," again, when her eyes went to a little bump that had suddenly sprung up under the bedclothes. She heard a sound – they both did – not a cry, more a sort of polite little cough.

The nurse went white in the face. She stripped back the bedclothes. Mrs Cuthbertson-Jones sat up and looked. They both goggled.

There in the bed was the prettiest, sweetest little baby either of them had ever seen or imagined.

The nurse gaped at it with her mouth hanging open. Then she threw one look of reproach at Mrs Cuthbertson-Jones, as if she had tricked her somehow, and scooped the baby up in her arms.

"Why didn't you TELL me?" she asked Mrs Cuthbertson-Jones.

"I did tell you." she replied, and then said, "Do let me hold the darling little creature."

The nurse was giving the baby a sponge-bath. As she did so, all her annoyance and hurt pride just melted away. She had never seen such a beautiful child in all her life. Just holding it and looking into its milky-blue eyes made the nurse feel calm and happy. She was very sorry when she had to hand it over to its mother. She had a curious feeling that she wanted to go on holding it for ever.

As soon as Mrs Cuthbertson-Jones had the baby in her arms, her pink cloud rose a little farther and she felt as if she had reached the gates of heaven and sailed right through them.

She knew at once that this was a very, very special baby.

Most babies, when they are first born, are all red and crinkled and they tend to scream and cry at finding themselves out in the world. But not this one.

This baby just lay in its mother's arms, gurgling and smiling.

"Look! A smile!" said the proud mother.

Since parting from the baby, the nurse had gone back to being herself again. "Nonsense," she said briskly. "Babies don't smile until they're several months old."

"This one does. Just you look."

The nurse glanced at the baby's face. Her eyes became fixed.

"Well! That is really extraordinary! She *is* smiling!"

"Oh! Is it a girl?" asked Mrs Cuthbertson-Jones, who hadn't thought to ask before.

"Yes, it's a dear – sweet – beautiful – perfect little girl," said the nurse, in a voice she herself hardly recognised, because it sounded like golden syrup. "Shall I go and find hubby and tell him?"

But before Mrs Cuthbertson-Jones could answer, her face changed.

"Ow!" she said suddenly. And before the nurse could do anything, she shouted "OW!" much louder than before.

The nurse whisked the baby away because Mrs Cuthbertson-Jones was now yelling and threshing about so much in the bed that she was afraid she might drop it.

"Whatever is the matter with you?" she asked crossly. "It's all over now!"

"NO IT ISN'T!" shouted Mrs Cuthbertson-Jones. "OW OW OW! It hurts, it HURTS!"

"You're just imagining—" began the nurse.

But suddenly she broke off, because under the bedclothes, which she'd pulled back up to keep the patient warm, something strange was happening.

Another bump had appeared!

But this time it didn't just lie there making a polite little cough. It looked as if the bump was punching and kicking. And no sooner had

Mrs Cuthbertson-Jones stopped yelling than the bump began to.

And what yells! The nurse was so astonished that for a few seconds she couldn't move. Never had she heard a new-born baby make such a noise – never!

She quickly recovered herself and pulled the covers back. Once again Mrs Cuthbertson-Jones sat up and looked.

They both reeled back at the sight that met their eyes.

A most hideous little baby lay there on its back, purple in the face, punching and kicking around it. Its mouth was wide open and its tiny eyes – eyes as green as the first baby's were blue – glittered with rage. It was screaming its head off.

Mrs Cuthbertson-Jones fell back on her pillows. Her pink cloud dissolved and fell to earth with a jolt. "Gracious me! What is it?"

"It's a baby, dear," said the nurse grimly. "Yes," she added to herself. "That's what it is. What else can it be? It's a baby."

"Let me hold it," whispered Mrs Cuthbertson-Jones bravely. "This one's my baby too."

"Very well, dear, if you're sure." She turned to pick the baby up. "UP-si-daisy!" she was saying, when it turned its head and bit her severely on the thumb.

The nurse dropped it with a shriek. Luckily – or perhaps unluckily – it fell back on to the bed and, apart from a small bounce, was unharmed.

The nurse was examining her thumb in amazement. It throbbed like snakebite.

"Toothmarks!" she muttered. "I don't believe this!"

She put on a pair of thick rubber gloves (she really wished they could have been gardening ones) and approached the baby again. This time she was careful, and although the baby twisted its face and tried to bite, the nurse had a firm hold of its head and it couldn't. It managed to get in a good kick in the nurse's stomach, though, and as soon as it could, it reached up its tiny hand, pulled her glasses off and began to gnaw them.

The nurse snatched them back, put the baby

on a table, held it down and looked into its mouth.

It had four sharp little teeth, two up and two down.

Still holding its head, the nurse felt its arms and legs. There seemed to be a lot of muscles in them. The baby was struggling to get free of her hands. She had to use a lot of strength to hold on to it.

She let her eyes go to the first baby, which was lying in a carry-cot on the table.

It lay there like a little rose, all pink and perfect, cooing and smiling and waving its tiny hands in the air.

She looked back at the baby she was holding.

It was even more hideous than when it had first been born. Its face was dark red, almost purple. The rest of it was a sort of blue. It had hair like puce corkscrews. It had long sharp finger- and toenails. It had stopped screaming and was glaring at her and grinding its four teeth.

The nurse had to hold down more than the baby. She was holding down a feeling of terror.

"Afraid of a baby?" she scolded herself. "Nonsense!"

Holding it firmly, she wiped it clean and wrapped it securely in a blanket. She had to fight against the feeling that she was tying it up.

"Are you sure you want to hold it, dear?" she asked the mother.

"Oh yes," said Mrs Cuthbertson-Jones faintly. "I think so. Don't I?"

"Well, I wouldn't," thought the nurse, "wouldn't want to touch it with a bargepole." But she handed it to Mrs Cuthbertson-Jones and felt extremely glad to get rid of it. She stripped off the rubber gloves and gave her hands a good wash. Blood was still pouring from her thumb.

Meanwhile Mrs Cuthbertson-Jones was trying to get over an uncomfortable feeling that she didn't like this baby nearly as much as the first one.

She knew it was absolutely wrong for a mother to feel like this, so she worked very hard on seeing the nice side of this one.

It wasn't easy. Certainly not while its little green eyes were open and glaring at her. But after a short time, it fell asleep. Its face became a little less purple. Its corkscrew hair stopped sticking out so much. Its hands and feet stopped struggling inside the tight blanket.

Mrs Cuthbertson-Jones stroked its cheek with one finger and thought she might be able to love it after all. At least, if it slept a lot.

The nurse was recovering from her shock and the pain in her thumb. She glanced at the baby and thought perhaps she hadn't been quite fair to it. It was certainly a most strange-looking infant, but after all, as she reminded herself, you can't expect to take to all of them.

Still, as she left the room, she couldn't shake off the feeling that she had taken part in something most unusual and – what was the word?

Sinister.

2. Babies

When Mr Cuthbertson-Jones first saw the babies, he felt quite overwhelmed. He had had no idea his wife was expecting twins, any more than she had.

"Please don't think I'm being silly," he said, "but... are you perfectly sure this one is ours?"

Mrs Cuthbertson-Jones was just about to say, "I'm afraid so," in an apologetic voice, but she changed it quickly. "Yes," she said meekly.

"Because sometimes there are mistakes – babies getting swopped—?" he said hopefully.

"No, dear. She is ours," said his wife.

"Oh. Oh well. I suppose we must just make the best of it," he said.

Mrs Cuthbertson-Jones felt upset, because it was all too clear that her husband had not taken to the second baby. But as she hadn't exactly decided what she felt about it either, she couldn't say much. And he was certainly overjoyed with the first one.

Various doctors, nurses and others came to look at the babies. Mrs Cuthbertson-Jones got used to the way they turned pale when they looked at the second baby, and how their faces broke into soppy smiles when they looked at the first.

Nobody thought it a good idea to tell Mrs Cuthbertson-Jones that the nurse who had attended the birth had only just been saved from bleeding to death from the bite on her thumb.

When she brought her babies home, Mrs Cuthbertson-Jones found that her husband had bought an extra cot and put it up in the little room they had prepared for the one baby they'd been expecting.

They put the babies into their cots and stood looking at them.

"What are we going to name them, dearest?" asked Mrs Cuthbertson-Jones timidly. Of course they had thought of lots of names in advance, but somehow they all seemed unsuitable now.

They went downstairs and consulted the baby-name book. They were soon able to settle on two nice names: Jill and Jane.

"Jill sounds so – so sunny," said Mrs Cuthbertson-Jones. "And Jane sounds so—"

"Ordinary," said Mr Cuthbertson-Jones hopefully. "Don't you think so, dear?"

It was as if wishing could make it so.

Two weeks passed.

Jill was a delight, a sheer delight. When her mother took her in her arms to feed her, she smiled sweetly at her, reached for the bottle, guided the teat to her little rosebud mouth, and drank all her milk. She brought up very little wind, and that in tiny pops. She never, ever cried.

Jane, on the other hand, screamed the entire time she was awake, which was about twenty hours out of every twenty-four.

When her mother – or, more often, her father, because he was stronger – would pick her up, she would thresh and kick and arch her back. When she felt the teat in her mouth she would clamp her teeth on it and bite it so hard that she got through one every feed. The milk spilt through the holes she made and almost choked her, making her scream louder than ever and blow the milk in all directions.

Once she bit the teat right off and swallowed it. She then threw up the bitten-off rubber teat and all the milk she'd swallowed, all over Mr Cuthertson-Jones, the best chair, the wallpaper and the new carpet.

The business of bringing up her wind is best not described.

Before long they decided they had better feed Jane outdoors, to save cleaning up. But that didn't work. The neighbours thought they were killing her and called the RSPCC. When the

RSPCC arrived, in the shape of a nice young woman, she took one look at Jane and decided cruelty to children might, in some cases, be justified.

After that Mr Cuthbertson-Jones tried feeding Jane in the bathroom.

Cleaning the room after every feed got very tiring for him. Not to mention cleaning himself. After a week, he decided the best thing was to get undressed to his underpants, get right into the bath, and feed Jane there. Later he found that standing under the shower in his underpants was even better. When the feed was over, he would turn on the shower and clean them both off, come out, change Jane into a dry nappy (not that it stayed dry for long), put her into her cot and then get dressed himself.

Then he usually had to get undressed again and go to bed for a rest. It was wearing him out.

Meanwhile his wife would be having a lovely, peaceful time with Jill.

It didn't seem fair to Mr Cuthbertson-Jones. But what could he do? He knew his wife could never manage Jane.

And, besides, he had begun silently wondering whether Jane might not be in some way *his fault*.

Mr Cuthbertson-Jones was not a bad man at all, but when he thought about it, he knew he had not led a blameless life. He had done wrong things sometimes. Perhaps Jane was his punishment? This thought, which he couldn't share with his wife for fear she might ask him *what* wrong things he had done, bothered him a lot.

One day he said to his wife, "We'll have to see about getting the girls christened, dear."

His wife did not reply at once. Later, when she had got her courage up, she said in a little trembly voice, "Do you really think the vicar will agree to baptise Jane?"

"Well, he'd better! It's his job, isn't it?" said Mr Cuthbertson-Jones quite angrily. The same thought had occurred to him, but when his wife said it, it upset him.

But he'd been thinking anyway about visiting the vicar. To talk about things like punishment.

The vicar was a small, mild-mannered man, with wispy hair, thick glasses and a sweet smile. He was a very good man; he saw the best in everyone, and the only thing wrong with him as a vicar was that he simply couldn't believe in evil, which vicars are definitely supposed to do.

Mr Cuthbertson-Jones went to see him alone.

"I want to book a christening," he said. "For our twin girls."

"How charming!" cried the vicar, beaming. "Two is twice as good as one, eh?"

"Er, yes," replied Mr Cuthbertson-Jones. "Usually. I mean, yes, if you say so."

The vicar took out his engagement book. "Next Tuesday suit you?" he asked. "Good! Three p.m? Good! Got the names all picked out?"

"Jill and Jane."

"Very nice indeed."

"Yes. Only I'm not sure they're suitable."

"Suitable? What do you mean?"

"They're such – ordinary names," muttered Mr Cuthbertson-Jones.

"And of course your little ones are not ordinary in your eyes! I understand!" said the vicar heartily.

Mr Cuthbertson-Jones changed the subject.

"Do you think God ever punishes us for doing wrong things?" he asked.

"Oh dear me," said the vicar, taking off his glasses and rubbing them with his hanky. "Why are we talking of awful things on this happy occasion?"

"I... I mean, might he punish a person by – that is, might he *send* a punishment, a sort of – burden to be borne?"

"Ah, we all have our burdens!" said the vicar cheerfully.

"Some heavier than others," said Mr Cuthbertson-Jones grimly.

3. The Christening

On the appointed Tuesday, Mr and Mrs Cuthbertson-Jones dressed the babies up in beautiful christening robes. They were the ones each of the parents had been christened in, when they were babies.

Jill was slipped into hers with no problem at all. She lay quite still while all the little buttons were done up and she looked enchanting in it.

Getting Jane into hers was another matter. She fought tooth and nail. So far her parents had managed not to get bitten by her, but bending over her to do the buttons, Mrs Cuthbertson-Jones got a long scratch on the nose, which was a pity on such an important day.

Jill's soft fair hair was smoothed down tenderly on her forehead.

Jane's hair stuck out in puce corkscrews around her face. She looked like someone in a comic-book who's had a terrible fright.

"Couldn't she wear a cap, dear?" asked Mr Cuthbertson-Jones.

His wife ran to get one of the little linen caps that came with the robes, but it was no use. The corkscrews were so stiff the cap wouldn't go on over them.

On the way to the church, Mr Cuthbertson-Jones drove and Mrs Cuthbertson-Jones sat in front with Jill in her arms. Jane was in the back in a carry-cot round which were wound yards of strong plastic twine. She was ominously quiet all the way to the church. When they arrived they found she had bitten through the twine in five places and got completely tangled up in it.

The godparents were waiting in the porch. Jill's godparents were Mrs Cuthbertson-Jones' sister and her husband. They were beaming all over their faces. They were the winners of a tremendous battle among all the relatives, as to who should be godparents to Jill. The godmother, who was dressed as if for a royal wedding, clucked and cooed and said she could hardly wait to take darling little Jilly in her arms.

Jane's godparents were there, too. Jill's godparents were standing quite far away from them because of the smell. Mr Cuthbertson-Jones had, in desperation, gone out the night before and found them sleeping under a bridge. They were both homeless and hungry and Mr Cuthbertson-Jones had paid them to come to the church.

He thought now that they might have tried to clean up a bit. He went up to them and asked

Jane's godmother quietly to please put her cigarette out and pull her hat farther down over her face. He begged Jane's godfather to hitch up his trousers and not to bring out the bottle of drink he could see bulging in his pocket, at least while they were in church.

There were quite a lot of people in the pews, and they all turned to look as Mr and Mrs Cuthbertson-Jones walked up the aisle to the font. The godparents followed, Mrs Cuthbertson-Jones' sister trying to keep as far as possible from Jane's godparents, who shuffled along behind, both reeking of drink and other things.

The vicar was waiting, all got up in his christening gear. He was smiling happily at the idea of baptising two sweet little children. He was certain it was going to be a wonderful occasion, but then, he always thought that.

When they were all standing around the font, the vicar said some prayers and then asked for the babies to be handed to him one at a time.

Jill was first. Mrs Cuthbertson-Jones gave her to her sister who clucked and cooed some more until the vicar gave a little cough and held out his arms.

"What name is to be given to this child?" he asked as he took her.

"Jillikins," gurgled the godmother.

"Jill. Just Jill," said the mother hastily.

The vicar held the baby in the proper manner, on a slant with its head down towards the water in the font. He cast his eyes up to heaven.

"I name this child—" he began. Then he looked down, and saw the baby's face for the first time. Its heavenly blue eyes were looking straight into his.

He gasped. For some moments there was complete silence.

Then the vicar did a thing he'd never done before. He clasped the baby to his heart and began to cry.

"Angela!" he sobbed.

"No! Jill!" cried both the parents. But it was too late. He had named the baby Angela, which of course means "Angel" in Latin, which all vicars are supposed to speak fluently. Most of them don't, but this one did.

When the hubbub had died down, and the two godparents had managed to pry Jill-now-Angela out of the vicar's arms, it was Jane's turn.

Reluctantly, Mr Cuthbertson-Jones turned to the other godmother, who stamped her cigarette out on the flagstones, coughed wetly, wiped the palms of her hands down the sides of her dirty old skirt and grabbed Jane, who was securely swaddled in a shawl so she couldn't use her nails.

The tramp-lady didn't bother looking at her godchild. She just thrust the bundle straight into the arms of the vicar and took another cigarette from behind her ear. The godfather meanwhile was furtively swigging from his bottle behind the nearest pillar.

The vicar looked like a person who has just opened the most wonderful present he has ever had in his life, and before even getting used to that, is given another.

"And what name is to be give to THIS divine and wondrous creature?" he asked with a smile of radiant happiness on his face.

"Jemima or somefin'," said the godmother.

Poor Mr and Mrs Cuthbertson-Jones were getting quite unnerved.

"JANE! JANE!" they shouted, so that everyone in the church jumped.

The vicar held the baby as before, looked up

to heaven with a seraphic smile, and began: "I name this baby—"

And then he looked down into a pair of glittering little green eyes.

This good and kindly man had never been able to believe that anyone could be really bad, let alone a tiny newborn baby. But now he saw for the very first time that he had been wrong.

The shock was so awful that he dropped the baby straight into the font, which was an old-fashioned, deep one.

She made a terrific splash, and disappeared under the water. Before anyone could move, she popped straight up again like a cork, and let out a shriek of outrage so loud that everyone around the font fell back, holding their ears.

At the end of this piercing shriek she had to take in a breath. In the silence while she did this, a single word, like a cry of anguish, pierced the church from end to end.

"*Diabola!*"

The vicar, unfortunately, was also fluent in Greek. Diabola means "evil one" in Greek. Coming from this good man, who had never sworn in his life, this terrible cry amounted to the worst word he had ever said.

But with it, he had named the baby.

4. Toddlers

Mr and Mrs Cuthbertson-Jones were rather religious. So, although they had really wanted their children to be called Jill and Jane, when the vicar christened them Angela and Diabola, they felt they couldn't go against it.

"Couldn't we call them Jill and Jane for short?" asked Mrs Cuthbertson-Jones wistfully.

"No, dear," said her husband, and added reasonably, "You see, Jill is not short for Angela, and Jane is not short for Diabola."

"Could we call them Angie and Di, then?" asked his wife.

Mr Cuthbertson-Jones thought about it. But it just didn't seem right. He was very keen to stay on the right side of God just then. He felt God must have put those two names into the vicar's mind.

"I think the vicar knew best, dear," he said at last.

The twins grew. Diabola grew faster than Angela. Much faster.

By the time they were a year old, Diabola was almost too big to lift. And that was awkward, because she crawled as fast as lightning. Very often the only way to stop her from doing whatever she was doing, was to pick her up.

This was not a safe thing to do.

She had a lot more teeth now. And she'd learnt, very early, how to spit. She did this with deadly accuracy. She was also very strong.

When she was one and a bit, the cat objected to having its tail pulled. It turned on Diabola, most unwisely, and bit her. She put both her chubby little hands round its neck and in three seconds it was dead.

Her parents found out about this at once. They happened to have stepped out into the garden for a moment, to have a private word about Diabola's spitting, and the dead cat came whirring out of the open French windows and hit Mr Cuthbertson-Jones with a thwack on the back of the head.

He stumbled forward into a flowerbed and when his wife helped him up, he was not only covered with earth and squashed begonias, he had the dead cat draped round his neck.

When Mrs Cuthbertson-Jones had stopped screaming, they buried the cat and Mr Cuthbertson-Jones said, "Well, perhaps it's for the best. It wasn't having an easy time. I'm afraid Diabola doesn't like animals."

They returned to the house and found Diabola about to poke her finger into an electric socket.

Now of course this is an extremely dangerous thing to do. But neither of them actually rushed to stop her, which afterwards they were to feel bad about. The thing was, they were still in shock about the cat.

However, incredibly, no harm came to her. When her finger made contact with the electricity there was a flash, and then there was Diabola, looking intently at the tip of her finger, which was fizzing and sparking. She put it in her mouth and sucked it.

Her parents didn't know if they imagined that all of a sudden her corkscrew curls stuck up at an even sharper angle than they usually did and took on a momentary tinge of electric blue.

Anyway she didn't seem to be any the worse, and immediately crawled to the nearest occasional table, pulled herself upright, and started throwing all the ornaments on it into the fireplace.

"Look, dear! Diabola can stand up!" said Mrs Cuthbertson-Jones proudly.

"Yes, I see she can," said her father grimly. "Just stop her throwing those things, will you, dear? I've got a headache."

And he left the room.

Mrs Cuthbertson-Jones hesitated, then approached Diabola – not too close – and put out her hand for a little china rabbit that had been a wedding present.

"Give it to Mumsy, Diabola dear!" she said brightly. "Don't throw – naughty!"

She should have known better. Whenever she said "Naughty!" to Diabola about anything, a fiendish smile spread over her face and she did – or went on doing – whatever it was, at once. This time she gave the china rabbit to Mumsy, as hard as she could throw.

Mrs Cuthbertson-Jones bent double and said "Ooof!" but she stopped the rabbit from falling to the floor, which she was very pleased about.

"Lost the cat, saved the rabbit," she said brightly to her husband later, trying to make light of it.

"Can't win 'em all," he said, taking another aspirin.

Meanwhile, Angela, too, had learnt to crawl and to stand up. She'd actually learnt to do both earlier than her sister. But whenever she did anything that Diabola couldn't do yet, Diabola got so – well, let's just say, upset – that her parents thought it best to keep the twins apart.

In their small house this grew more and more difficult, and Angela had some rather narrow escapes.

The Cuthbertson-Joneses did their best to make the house child-proof. They kept doors and windows closed, they hid everything that could be thrown or dropped, and everything sharp (that was after they caught Diabola using her mother's nail-scissors to try to cut her sister's nails – right off).

But Diabola had ideas nobody else would have thought of. It was only because the clothes-basket was so heavy that Mrs Cuthbertson-Jones found out in time that Diabola had hidden a sleeping Angela amid the dirty clothes that were just going to be put in the washing-machine.

These incidents were quite apart from all the casual attempts Diabola made to pinch, punch, kick, bite or hit Angela over the head.

In the end, the parents made a big decision.

They turned their own bedroom into a room for Angela. They moved her cot in there and all her things.

Mr and Mrs Cuthbertson-Jones moved into the living-room where they slept on a sofa-bed. It was really a big sacrifice, but they did it gladly, for Angela's sake.

It became necessary to arrange strong nylon netting tightly over the top of Diabola's cot (now reinforced with metal bars) and to sound-proof the whole thing as best they could without suffocating her.

Angela never got into any mischief or did anything naughty at all. She crawled about, and played nicely with her teddies and dolls, scribbled very talentedly in her colouring books, and showed an interest in proper books too. She soon learnt to make all the right animal noises to go with the pictures, baaing and clucking and quacking and mooing.

The girls hadn't been together for some time. They didn't have meals together or go out together. As their parents put it, "It just doesn't work."

The parents took it in turns to take Angela out in her pram or to the shops. It was a thrill that never faded to watch people's reactions. When strangers looked at her they seemed to come over all peculiar. Old ladies stroked her hair, which was now a mass of soft curls. Tough young men made silly noises and asked if they could kiss her. Women with babies of their own took one look, and whirled their prams around, making off as fast as they could before envy got the better of them.

The parents seldom took Diabola out. Because even when she'd been very small, when people looked at her, they gasped, put their hands over their eyes or mouths, and backed away.

So the only fresh air Diabola got was out in the garden, where she crawled about rapidly, pulled the heads off flowers, frightened the birds and, if someone didn't watch her closely, dug up cat's-mess.

If Diabola happened to find anything of Angela's, she would try to destroy it on the spot.

That's why their parents were so astonished when one day Angela spoke her first words. They were, "Where Dybo?"

It had never occurred to either of her parents that she might be missing her twin sister.

But they both believed in answering children's questions truthfully. So Mrs Cuthbertson-Jones said, "Diabola is locked in her room, dear."

"Why?" was Angela's next word.

"Because Mummy's tired," was the truthful answer.

"Poor Mum-mum. Poor Dybo," Angela said sweetly.

That was the whole conversation, for the moment. Both her parents thought that these enquiries showed that Angela had an extraordinarily loving and caring nature.

Which she had.

The problem was Diabola's nature. This was not merely *un*loving and *un*caring, but the complete opposite of Angela's.

Diabola's nature could best be described as hateful, spiteful, destructive, vindictive, repulsive, and many other "-fuls" and "-ives". Plus some "-somes" and "-ings" as well, such as loath*some* and disgust*ing*.

But just *how* -ful, -ive, -some and -ing she was, her parents had yet to learn.

Poor things. Little did they know what lay ahead!

5. Shopping

One day, there was shopping to be done.

It was Mr Cuthbertson-Jones's turn to take Angela. He got her dressed in a pretty romper-suit. Since Angela never dribbled or got dirty, her clothes always looked spotless and she didn't need others until she grew out of them, whereupon they were taken to Oxfam where they were sold as new.

When she was ready, Mr Cuthbertson-Jones crept out with her by the back door. Mrs Cuthbertson-Jones, who knew the routine, had Diabola with her in the kitchen, where she had given her some rotten fruit and eggs, specially kept for her till they went bad, to squash, sit on, smear herself with, and throw about.

It was much easier to let her do some of the things she liked if they were not too awful, than try to stop her all the time. Mind you, the eggs were pretty awful. Of course they were Diabola's favourite rotten thing to squash and throw, and her mother had to be quick on her feet.

Mr Cuthbertson-Jones had just settled Angela in her pushchair (she didn't need to be strapped in, of course, she just sat there holding the sides and smiling around her at everything) when Angela suddenly said, "Want Dybo come too."

"OH NO!" her father groaned before he could stop himself. "Not that! You can't mean it, Angela!"

For the first time ever, the happy smile faded from Angela's face. She certainly didn't frown or scowl or anything like that, but just to see her face without its smile nearly broke her father's heart.

"P'ease, Da-da," she said in a tiny, but irresistible, voice.

With great reluctance, Mr Cuthbertson-Jones returned to the house. He went into the kitchen (which was by now stinking to high heaven of rotten eggs) and said, in the hollow tones of a man bound for execution, "Dear, Angela wants Diabola to go shopping with us."

His wife stared at him with her mouth open. But she knew that if Angela wanted it, they must do it.

Diabola, who had been just about to throw a putrid tomato at her father, stopped with her hand in mid-air, looked from one parent to the other, and waited.

With one accord, both of them swooped down and seized her. This was generally the only way they could move her – they had to take her by surprise and subdue her between them.

They carried her to the bathroom where they stripped off her filthy, smelly clothes and held her under the shower. Then they dried and dressed her in a clean outfit, and trussed her up with Mr Cuthbertson-Jones's university scarf. They were carrying her between them to the back door, when they realised something.

They had no need to hold her so tight. She wasn't struggling. She wasn't screaming. She wasn't kicking or trying to bite.

She hadn't spat at them once.

They looked at each other in bewilderment.

"Perhaps you could go alone, dear," said Mrs Cuthbertson-Jones hopefully. "While I clean up the kitchen."

But Mr Cuthbertson-Jones was taking no chances.

"No, dear," he said firmly. "You must come too. We'll go—" he swallowed, "—as a family."

Tears came into both their eyes. But Mrs Cuthbertson-Jones nodded.

They strapped Diabola into her own push chair and attached it to Angela's.

"Do you think we should untie her, dear? People might think—"

"No! No!" shouted her father, and then tried to calm himself. "Let's just see how it goes, shall we?"

He had reason to be nervous.

The last time he had taken Diabola shopping, she had thrown the whole store into turmoil. While reducing her father to a state of helpless nerves with continuous shrieking, she had reached out of the trolley into the fruit display, hurled oranges at passers-by, pulled a yucca plant out of its pot, and when the manager had been called, hit him on the head with a well-aimed tin of pineapple. On their way out, she had spat at the check-out girl and sent her into hysterics. Her father still shuddered at the memory.

This time, however, things might perhaps be different.

The twins, who hadn't seen each other properly for months, sat side by side in their pushchairs and stared into one another's eyes. Both were perfectly silent all the way to the supermarket. Their parents, on tenterhooks, wheeled the double pushchair between them and held their breaths until their faces turned blue.

At the door of the store, they braced themselves.

"Are you ready, dear?"

"Yes, dear, if you are."

"Just... just... be prepared."

"I am, dear."

"For *anything*."

"Yes. There are two of us, don't forget!"

"I do love you, dear," said Mr Cuthbertson-Jones unexpectedly.

They marched into the store, both holding the handles of the pushchairs.

They transferred the two little girls to two separate trolleys, and sat them in the special seats for children.

They kept the university scarf wrapped tightly around Diabola. She looked like a large stripy cocoon. Her head with its spiky hair stuck out at the top. Her eyes were fastened on her sister in the next trolley.

They did the frozen-food shopping together,

side by side. People smiled besottedly at Angela as usual, glanced at the stripy cocoon that was Diabola, grimaced, and moved hastily away. Nothing worse happened, and Mr Cuthbertson-Jones began to feel braver.

"You go to the fruit and veg section, dear, and I'll go to the biscuits and tea section," said Mr Cuthbertson-Jones. "It'll save time."

"Very well, dear," said his wife meekly. She turned Angela's trolley and went round the end of the aisle. The moment she was out of sight, Mr Cuthbertson-Jones froze in his tracks. A sound he had never heard before rent the air.

It was Angela. She was *crying*.

Mr Cuthbertson-Jones abandoned Diabola and rushed round the corner. His wife was standing beside Angela's trolley, transfixed, staring at Angela, who was bawling quite as loudly as ever Diabola had. Mr Cuthbertson-Jones snatched her from the trolley, almost pulling her feet off, and began rocking her violently.

"Angela, Angela!" he cried distractedly. "What's wrong, sweetheart, what is it? Oh, do stop, I can't bear it!"

All around, people began to gather and stare. Mrs Cuthbertson-Jones stood motionless with tight-shut eyes, imagining herself deep underground.

"Take her outside and try to calm her down!" cried Mr Cuthbertson-Jones, distraught. "That sound! I can't stand it!" He thrust Angela into his wife's arms and rushed up the dog-and-cat-food aisle like a madman.

Mrs Cuthbertson-Jones tried to soothe Angela, but she couldn't. Angela kept crying, and pointing. At last her mother understood.

"Do you want Diabola?" she whispered in her daughter's ear.

The awful crying stopped as if by a switch. Angela's pearly smile appeared like sunlight through clouds.

"Dybo!" she cried happily. "Shoppies with Dybo!"

Her mother dumped her back in the trolley-seat and whizzed it round the corner.

There she stopped dead.

The crowd she had left in the dog-and-cat-food aisle was as nothing to the crowd that had gathered in the tinned food and condiments aisle.

Of course it had been madness to leave Diabola alone for a single moment. Especially with a trolley half-full of frozen foods. Even in a cocoon. Diabola had lost not a second in wrenching herself free of the soft stretchy scarf, and was now standing up in the trolley, hurling well-directed frozen chicken pieces in all directions.

So deadly was her aim and so swift her movements that no one dared approach her. You could hardly see her little arms – they were just a blur, and the chicken pieces were a blur too, until they came to a stop against their targets. People who had gathered to watch, were soon screaming and fleeing.

Before Mrs Cuthbertson-Jones could do anything, the chicken pieces ran out. With one swift double-handed movement, Diabola ripped open a packet of frozen fish fillets, and began hurling them about like boomerangs.

These were much more dangerous than the

blunt chicken pieces. One woman barely saved her child from decapitation by catching the flying fillet in her hand like a frisbee, and throwing it straight back at Diabola.

It caught Diabola a stinging blow on her throwing wrist. She dropped the bag of fish fillets and fell on her face in the trolley, clutching her wrist and gathering herself for a screech of fury.

Mrs Cuthbertson-Jones gasped and, forgetting all danger, threw herself forward.

"How dare you throw a frozen fish fillet at my child!" she cried, giving the woman a strong push. "You might have cut her hand off!"

"Is that little monster yours?" shouted the outraged woman from a sitting position on the floor. "She's a menace to the public! And so are you, you – monster's mother! Call the manager!"

This cry was taken up by a dozen voices. Customers and assistants alike were cowering behind displays or crouched behind their trolleys, and their shouts brought the manager running. And not just the manager. The check-out girl who had been spat at by Diabola last time had noticed her going in, and with great presence of mind had already summoned the police.

It took two policewomen and the manager (who well remembered her last visit) to subdue her. One policewoman and the manager ran round her in opposite directions, each holding one end of the scarf till she was a cocoon again.

Meanwhile, the other policewoman put the distraught Mrs Cuthbertson-Jones under close arrest.

6. The Vicar Does His Best

Mrs Cuthbertson-Jones was had up before a magistrate.

The couple had had to bring the twins with them to court. The magistrate kept staring at them and it clouded his judgement. One moment he would be looking at Angela and thinking that any woman with a child like that couldn't be guilty of anything. The next he would glance at Diabola and want to put her mother away for life.

Unfortunately Diabola was the last one he looked at, so he jailed Mrs Cuthbertson-Jones for a month.

Afterwards he couldn't sleep for thinking that if he'd only been allowed to send Diabola to prison too, he would probably have got a knighthood for it.

Poor Mr Cuthbertson-Jones of course blamed himself, and perhaps rightly. He should never have run away and left his wife in charge of both twins. But now he had his own punishment, because while his wife was in jail he was left to cope with the twins.

He farmed Angela out to the neighbours, who were dying to look after her, while he struggled alone with Diabola. He had to spend every waking hour with her.

He'd been working from home for some time, but now he couldn't work at all, and within a week he'd lost his job.

He missed his wife terribly and could hardly bear to think of her in prison, but he was too busy even to visit her.

Mr and Mrs Cuthbertson-Jones had both been firm believers in talking to babies, but it had been difficult to do this with Diabola. They didn't dare to reproach her, no matter what she did. On the other hand, they couldn't very well praise her. And ordinary remarks such as "Time for din-dins" or "Diabola want the potty?" not to mention games like "Incy-wincy spider" and "This little piggy went to market" hardly seemed suitable.

But now Mr Cuthbertson-Jones was so lonely with his wife away in jail that he began to talk to Diabola without being able to help himself.

For instance, he would say, when he lifted the nylon netting off her cot in the mornings:

"Well, Diabola, so you've been tearing up your bedclothes again. We'll have to get you some canvas sheets and an asbestos blanket. Had a nice gnaw on the bars of your cot? That's fine, it'll wear down your teeth a bit. Well, come on then, I'll lasso you and put you in the big cage."

(Lassoing was a new skill he had had to acquire, because Diabola had learnt to race from one end of her cot to the other, ducking and weaving. "The big cage" was a device they had thought of when Diabola had first learnt to walk. It was like a tall playpen, only it was a cage with a barred lid, made of strong light-weight metal of the sort they make space-rockets out of.)

Diabola would stand in the cage, holding the metal bars, following her father about with her unblinking little green eyes. If he stopped talking for a while she would shake the bars and shout, "Daddy talk! Talk a-Dybo NOW! TALK TALK TALK!"

He tried. When he couldn't any more, he put on Radio 4. If there was a play on with lots of sound effects (sirens, shouting, shooting and screams), she might listen to that, but not for long. He tried music. Heavy metal seemed to soothe her, but Mr Cuthbertson-Jones loathed heavy metal and could only stand so much of it.

He tried every known game and distraction, unbolting the lid of the cage and dropping toys, books and games in to her, but she either tore them to bits at once or if she couldn't do that, she banged them against the bars. Then she would shout and yell: "Dybo WANT! Gimme! Gimme! Gimme!" But she never gave a hint of what she wanted. Until one day her father was wearily doing some cooking and she suddenly screamed: "Gimme! Ose! Gimme OSE!"

Her father didn't know what she wanted. "These? These?" he kept saying, pointing to this and that. She responded with cries of "NO NO TOOPID DADDY – OSE!" It wasn't till in desperation he pointed to the saucepans on the stove that he was rewarded. She rattled the bars and shrieked "ES!"

Something basically kind and patient in her father snapped.

"If you can say 'stupid' you can say 'pots'!" he barked. "Do you think I'm a mind-reader?"

Diabola stopped screeching and stared at him with her mouth open. He bent to the cupboard under the sink and took out two large saucepans. He got the lids out so she could bang them and took the top off the cage. She stood up ready to grab the pans from him, but something came over him.

He said, "Diabola, if you snatch, I won't give them to you."

She snatched anyway.

"Right," he said. "That's it!" And he slammed down the lid of the cage and bolted it.

Her face at once turned purple with rage and

she opened her mouth wide. But before she could draw breath he shouted, "Go on, scream, I'm used to it, I don't even hear it any more! I'm going outside anyway so you can scream your head off!"

He'd reached the stage where he was past caring if he upset her. He was too upset himself. He stamped off into the garden and dug a flowerbed furiously. He was so lonely and distraught, he forgot where they'd buried the cat, and found he'd dug it up. When he saw its bones and remembered how it had met its end, he hurled the spade at the wall, sat down on the grass and ground his teeth.

After a while he noticed that apart from the grinding, the only sound he could hear was birdsong.

He leapt up and rushed back into the kitchen.

Diabola was sitting silently in the cage with her back to him.

"Diabola, what's the matter?" her father asked. "Why aren't you screaming?"

Diabola turned her head slowly.

He gasped.

Her eyes were narrowed to slits that gleamed like green glass. She looked as if she'd like to do to him what she'd done to the cat.

For the first time, the very first time, Mr Cuthbertson-Jones felt seriously frightened of her. He backed away.

"Diabola," he said faintly. "I'm your father!"

She bared her teeth at him in a silent snarl.

He went to the phone and phoned the vicar.

"Please come at once," he said hoarsely. "I need help."

The vicar was not very busy. Not many people came to his church. He was glad of a call on his services. It made him feel useful and needed. He hurried over to the Cuthbertson-Joneses' house.

Mr Cuthbertson-Jones silently led him through into the kitchen.

Diabola was lying on the floor of the cage, fast asleep, with her head turned away.

"Good gracious!" exclaimed the vicar. "Why do you keep the poor child in a cage?"

"Vicar," said Mr Cuthbertson-Jones, "do you remember christening her? She is the baby you christened 'Diabola'."

The vicar gave a start. He had suppressed the memory of that terrible moment.

"Do – do you mean, you actually call her that?"

"It suits her very well," said Mr Cuthbertson-Jones, who had looked it up.

"You are not trying to tell me that that little innocent child—"

"She is not a little innocent child. She's a fiend."

The vicar didn't want to believe this. He approached the cage.

"Poor little thing," he murmured.

"She is not," said Mr Cuthbertson-Jones stonily, "a poor little thing. Ask me where her mother is."

"Where is her mother?"

"She's in jail."

The vicar started again. "Jail! But that's awful! What did she do?"

"She defended Diabola in a store. Of course it was other people who needed the defending, really," said Mr Cuthbertson-Jones wearily, and he told the vicar the story. He told him some other stories too. In fact the two of them sat in the kitchen and drank a lot of tea and the vicar heard all about the twins, everything their father could think of that might convince him that his help was needed.

"Let me get this straight," said the vicar at last. "Are you asking me to expel the evil from this child?"

"Yes."

"It goes against everything I believe."

"What do you mean? Surely as a man of

religion, you believe in good and evil?"

"No," said the vicar. "Not exactly. About people, I believe the old rhyme."

"What old rhyme is that?"

The vicar quietly recited:

"'There's so much good in the worst of us,
And so much bad in the best of us,
It ill-behoves any of us
To criticise the rest of us.'"

Mr Cuthbertson-Jones said, "That's all very nice. But my daughters are the exception. I can't go on, vicar. My wife is in prison and I've lost my job and my daughter terrifies me and you have to help."

At this moment, Diabola woke up, rolled over, and looked at the vicar.

The vicar stared at her for a moment. His blood seemed to freeze. Then he turned to the unhappy father, gave a small trembling nod, and left the house.

He hurried back to the vicarage.

"Mother in jail! Father desperate! And those eyes – those eyes!" He shuddered, remembering the baby he'd dropped into the font.

Still, he couldn't help feeling quite excited. He'd never done anything like this before. He'd never expected to. But it was part of the job, and he determined to do his best.

He returned with a whole lot of gear. He had a bell, a Bible, some chalk, several candles, and a huge bunch of herbs he'd picked in his garden. He wasn't sure which were the important ones so he'd just taken a good handful of all of them. He'd also had a quick look though some of his books, to refresh his memory. What he read struck him as rather melodramatic. He hoped he wouldn't feel silly when the time came.

When he got back into the house he found the other child – the heavenly one – was there, too. Mr Cuthbertson-Jones had gone next door and fetched her.

As soon as he saw her, the vicar felt his heart doing flip-flops.

"Oh, she's so beautiful!" he crooned. "Such a sweet, darling, perfect—"

"Yes," said Mr Cuthbertson-Jones shortly. "And when we've finished with Diabola, I want to talk to you about *her*."

Before the vicar could reply, Angela, sitting in her high chair, crowing and smiling and waving at Diabola, cried clearly, "Luvvie Dybo!"

The vicar started back. "She... she loves her sister?"

"Angela loves everyone," said Mr Cuthbertson-Jones wearily.

"May I have a word?" asked the vicar, frowning.

They went outside and closed the door.

"If one of them is perfectly good and one is perfectly bad, it couldn't possibly happen that the good one would love the bad one."

"Why not?"

"Why not? Because – because – don't you see? Good cannot love evil! It's against all the rules!"

Mr Cuthbertson-Jones had been trying to recover his snapped patience but he had failed.

"Don't tell me about rules!" he almost shouted. "Just do something!"

They returned to the kitchen.

The vicar drew the curtains. He lit the candles. He drew crosses on the floor (this was his own idea). He strewed herbs about. He rang his bell. He read some prayers as best he could by candlelight

(Mr Cuthbertson-Jones produced a large torch, which helped a bit). He even danced around the cage and got Mr Cuthbertson-Jones – who was prepared to stand on his head in a bucket of water and have the vicar set fire to his shoes, if necessary – to dance around too.

Diabola added to the strange atmosphere by uttering bursts of laughter. As she had never been known to laugh before, this was very unnerving to her father (not to say offputting to the vicar).

The vicar at last came to the climax of his ritual.

"Thou fiendish thing!" he cried. "Spawn of Beelzebub, leave the body of this hapless child and go thy ways!"

The vicar was straining every nerve. He was so carried away that he half expected Diabola's mouth to open and a stream of screaming ectoplasm to come forth.

But it didn't. Nothing happened at all. Diabola just sat there grinning with her eyes reflecting the candlelight.

The vicar's blood was up by now.

"Begone, vile spirit!" he cried dramatically. "Return to wherest thou belongeth!"

Diabola chuckled and clapped her hands. "Funny man," she said approvingly.

His pride in tatters, the vicar turned away and wiped his forehead.

"I'm sorry," he said grimly. "I seem to have failed dismally." He blew out the candles and opened the curtains.

"What about Angela?" panted Mr Cuthbertson-Jones.

"What about her?"

"Can't you do something about her?"

"Do what?"

"Get rid of some of her goodness!"

"WHAT? What are you saying?" asked the vicar in shocked tones.

"You said it yourself. She's perfect. Nobody should be perfect. I want her to be normal and ordinary and have faults like other people."

The vicar stared at him for a long moment. Then he turned away and started packing up his things.

"There is nothing in Scripture about getting rid of goodness," he said firmly.

Poor Mr Cuthbertson-Jones looked about him in desperation.

"So you can't do anything," he said. "That's what it comes to. You're useless."

"I've long suspected as much," said the vicar shortly. "I'm sorry."

He went to the back door with his gear under his arm. He hadn't bothered to clear up the herbs and the chalk marks. He just hadn't the heart.

As he left, Diabola laughed horribly.

Angela said ecstatically, "Dybo happy!"

"Well, I'm not!" thought Mr Cuthbertson-Jones. He was almost certain he never would be again.

7. Growing Up

There's no need to relate every event in the difficult years that followed for the Cuthbertson-Joneses.

People do manage. That's the strange thing. They think they can't, that their difficulties are so great that they will never get through. But somehow the days go by and – give or take a jail sentence, a nervous breakdown, lost friends, relatives who move away, jobs found, lost, replaced, endless rows with the social services, bouts of hysterics and hundreds of sleepless nights and headache pills – somehow, the years pass.

Angela and Diabola survived. So did their parents.

How? Did they have some secret weapon?

Well, the Cuthbertson-Joneses found out something. It made it just possible for them to carry on.

It was this: *the twins needed each other*. It was when they had to be separated that the worst things happened. When they could see and talk to each other, things were – well, things were dreadful, unspeakable, impossible, unbearable. But survivable, somehow.

The twins were like two magnets. If you put magnets together, sometimes they attract and rush to each other. If you turn them, they repel and you can't force them to touch. The twins were something like that.

They slept in the same room now. It was their parents' old room. It had had some adjustments made to it. Half of it was fenced off with bars. It was a large version of the "big cage". There was a gate that could be opened. At certain times, it could even be left open, and Diabola could come out and be with Angela, who occupied the other half of the room. That was during the "attract" times. When "repel" times happened, Diabola had to be put back into the barred part of the room and the gate padlocked.

At the top of the cage, up near the ceiling, was a roll of special stuff. It could be unrolled at the pull of a rope, rather like a blind.

That plunged Diabola into darkness and muffled her shrieks.

She didn't mind the dark but she did mind being left alone to yell. After a short time the noise would stop. Her parents would quickly roll up the special stuff again and say cheerfully, "Feeling better, Diabola? That's good!" In this way they taught her not to scream too much.

Diabola wasn't stupid.

Neither was Angela.

Angela wanted Diabola to be with her. Even when they were small, Angela offered her all her toys and didn't get upset when, as used to happen, Diabola promptly destroyed them or threw them at Angela or straight through the nearest window.

Instead, she stopped offering them, and waited till Diabola was locked up (but watching her sister through the bars) and then she would play nicely with her toys. After a while, Diabola got the idea: toys weren't just something to demolish. They were something to be played with.

So sometimes she played. Then things could be quite peaceful – for a bit. But Diabola had a very short attention span. Around two and a quarter minutes.

But that was before she found out about drawing.

One day she'd been watching Angela drawing on her scribbling pad. Angela loved drawing and was good at it. She would get so absorbed, she would forget all about Diabola, and if there was one thing Diabola could not stand (actually there were very many things like that) it was being forgotten about. She started to screech.

Angela turned to her and handed her her

pencil and a sheet of paper through the bars.

Diabola grabbed them, put the paper on the floor, and screeching all the time, stabbed the pencil at it forcibly until it broke.

But then she stopped screeching, and just stared down at the paper.

The marks on it were just from the jabbing. They didn't amount to a drawing of any kind. But Diabola seemed to see something there that appealed to her.

She thrust her hand out to Angela, who put a crayon into it.

Very cautiously, Diabola put the point of the crayon to the paper and made a mark. Then another. She looked up at Angela with a narrow, cunning look. She drew a circle, with some small circles inside it. She scribbled around it. A slow smile came over her face.

After a short time she let out a kind of cackle, and held up the paper. She liked what she saw. She made a few more marks and cackled again. She turned the paper round and showed it to Angela.

What Angela saw was a horrid face. It had crossed eyes and a splatty nose and sharp teeth and hair everywhere and a thoroughly nasty, mean expression. Yet somehow she knew it was meant to be her. It was how Diabola saw her. How Diabola wanted her to be.

After that, things got more peaceful for longer. And Mr and Mrs Cuthbertson-Jones were deceived into thinking that perhaps Diabola was growing out of her awfulness.

When Mrs Cuthbertson-Jones' birthday was approaching, Mr Cuthbertson-Jones made a rash decision.

He and his wife had been having a rough time. They were both worn out. It had been years since they'd been out together. But Mr Cuthbertson-Jones decided enough was enough. They would go out together for the birthday if he could possibly arrange things.

He had an uncle who was a retired army sergeant-major. He rang him up.

"Uncle Jocko," he began. "I want to take my wife out for a birthday treat."

"So what's your problem, old boy?"

"It's our twins. We need... we need a baby-sitter. A rather – special one."

"Had five nippers of my own. I'm your man!"

"One of our girls is a bit—"

"Bit of a handful, is she? Don't you worry! I know how to manage kids! Just name the day and leave the rest to me."

When the day came, Uncle Jocko arrived on the doorstep. He was six foot four with shoulders as wide as the front of a bus, size 13 boots and fists like bunches of bananas. He towered over the Cuthbertson-Joneses and could have picked up a twin in each hand. In fact that's just what he did, and tossed them about in playful fashion.

Angela quite enjoyed this. Diabola did not. But she was too surprised to do anything. At first.

Mrs Cuthbertson-Jones, who had refused to get dressed up to go out because she was quite sure she wouldn't be going, took one look at Uncle Jocko and ran to get ready.

Mr Cuthbertson-Jones gave Uncle Jocko his instructions, and then added, "We'll be back before bedtime. You won't leave them alone, will you? You'll stick with them all evening?"

"We're going to have a party of our own here!" chortled Uncle Jocko in his big sergeant-major voice. The twins stared at him.

As soon as Mr and Mrs Cuthbertson-Jones had left the house, Uncle Jocko went into his act.

He knew what kids like. A good laugh, that's what. And Uncle Jocko believed he was just the person to give it to them.

He sat the twins side by side on the sofa. "Now my little kiddiwinks, just keep your eye on Uncle Jocko!" he said heartily.

He opened a little suitcase he'd brought. Inside were all kinds of fun things. First of all, Uncle Jocko put a clown's hat on, and then a red clown's nose. Then he pulled out a big baggy pair of trousers with purple spots and put them on. Then he pulled lots of funny faces and fell down on his bottom several times.

Angela laughed, though in a rather embarrassed fashion.

Diabola's face remained stony.

Uncle Jocko kept waiting for her to laugh, and when she didn't, he took out a balloon and blew it up. First he let the air out of it twice, making a ruder noise each time, but when that didn't raise a laugh, he tied it to a stick, and after cavorting around the room a bit making "yoo-hoo-boomps-a-daisy!" noises, bopped Diabola on the head with the balloon.

Diabola in a lightning movement seized the balloon, burst it with her teeth, grabbed the end of the stick and thrust the other end up Uncle Jocko's rather large nose. Right through the red clown's one.

Uncle Jocko howled and hopped around the room, clutching his nose and bumping into things. Diabola finally decided that he *was* a funny man and began rolling on her back and screaming with laughter.

Uncle Jocko stopped howling and hopping and turned to look at her. Anyone else would have frozen at that look, which had terrified young soldiers when Uncle Jocko had been training them. But Diabola only pointed at his large angry face with the shattered remains of the clown's nose on it and laughed louder than ever.

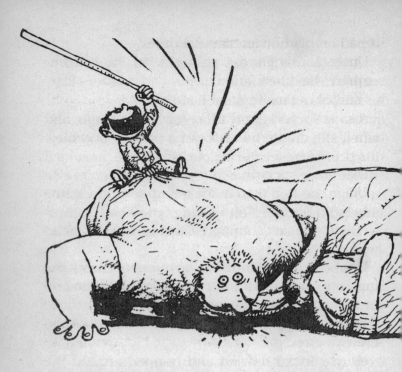

Angela slipped off the sofa and crawled under it instead, rather like someone going into an air-raid shelter when there is going to be a war.

Uncle Jocko dropped to his knees and peered under the sofa.

"Come out, Angie-girl!" he urged. "Dusty under there—" But he got no further. Diabola took one look at his large, purple-spotted rear-end sticking invitingly in the air. She picked up the stick, which he had pulled out of his nose, jumped onto his back and began whacking him like a horse, still laughing maniacally.

Uncle Jocko fell flat on his face, more from surprise than pain. Then he jumped up (very fast for such a big man), snatched the stick, hurled it across the room, and picked Diabola up in his ham-like fist. He didn't toss her about playfully this time, he gave her a good shake.

Diabola went limp and silent.

Uncle Jocko stopped. He held her out in front of him. She appeared to be unconscious.

"Blimey, what've I done?" muttered poor Uncle Jocko.

He laid Diabola on the sofa and bent over her. Angela, who had put her head out from under the sofa-frill, disappeared again.

Diabola came to abruptly as Uncle Jocko's face came within reach and gave him two black eyes, one with each tiny, but powerful, fist.

Uncle Jocko fell on his bottom for real.

When he clambered to his feet, he had a look on his face which, if he had been on an army parade-ground with a bunch of squaddies in front of him, would have sent them fleeing in all directions. But Diabola just sat calmly on the sofa waiting for him.

Mr and Mrs Cuthbertson-Jones didn't get much past the first course of their dinner out.

A waiter came hurrying over to them just as

they were deciding whether to have the Pizza Margherita or the Tagliatelle Carbonara to follow their delicious garlic bread.

"You're wanted on the telephone, Signore," he said. "Eet sound-a very urgent!"

Of course after listening to a spluttering, gasping, fuming Uncle Jocko for a few moments, there was nothing for Mr Cuthbertson-Jones to do but hurry back to the table, collect his wife and go home as fast as possible.

There is no need to detail the sight that met their eyes. Diabola had really taken a great dislike to Uncle Jocko... It's enough to say that Mr and Mrs Cuthbertson-Jones gave up any idea of ever going out together, and that Uncle Jocko never baby-sat for them (or, indeed, anyone else, even his own grandchildren) ever again.

When the twins had really begun to talk, they developed a strange language that their parents couldn't make head or tail of. Mr and Mrs Cuthbertson-Jones called this language Twinnish.

Diabola's half of talking Twinnish was, to begin with, mainly shrieks, snarls and gargling noises. Then swear-words were added. (Where did she hear them? Not from her parents, who were too religious to swear. She just seemed to know them.) But gradually she began to learn words from Angela, who spoke Twinnish as if she'd invented it. As, indeed, she must have done.

Angela talked regular English too, to her parents. Diabola now refused to talk anything but Twinnish, so Angela translated.

Diabola would say something, of which only the swear-words could be understood. It sounded something like "Ag gug grubble ig POOP-damn crapola bog-woggle". Then Angela would smile sweetly, and say, "Dybo wants her dinner now, please," or "Dybo says she wants to watch TV."

Angela, by the way, *never* called Diabola Diabola, only Dybo. As to what Diabola called Angela, she had many names for her, but they were all in Twinnish. Once, Mrs Cuthbertson-Jones ventured to ask Angela what Diabola called her.

Angela, who was four at the time, said, "Dybo calls me lots of names."

"Like what, for instance?"

"Today she's calling me Stinkpants," said Angela with an angelic smile.

Her mother, shocked, said, "That's not very nice!"

Angela replied, promptly but bafflingly, "*Dybo*'s not very nice. That's why I love her."

8. Little Girls at School

The time came for the twins to begin school.

Their parents talked endlessly about it. Both of them had been secretly dreaming of a time when the twins would be out of the house for several hours a day, and they could have a little time to themselves. But they both knew in their hearts it couldn't come true – not for long.

"What shall we tell the school?" asked Mrs Cuthbertson-Jones anxiously. "We can't not warn them!"

"They'll find out for themselves, soon enough," said Mr Cuthbertson-Jones grimly.

"They'll expel her on the first day," said his wife sadly. "She'll do something dreadful and that will be that."

On the first day of school, they got the twins dressed in their little uniforms, gave them each a little schoolbag and a little lunchbox, and then walked them along the road to the school.

By the time they arrived, Diabola had managed to tear her clothes and make her hands, legs and face filthy. She didn't want to go to school (unlike Angela who couldn't wait).

Several times she had let herself fall to the ground, nearly pulling her father's arm off, and had to be dragged along till they could hoick her to her feet and persuade her to walk a few more steps. She didn't scream or cry, but they could see her building up for a mighty explosion as soon as she could do it where her parents would be most shamed and embarrassed.

At the school door, Angela turned and said something in Twinnish to Diabola. Diabola uttered a curse. Then Angela did something she hardly ever did. She touched her sister.

Their parents stiffened and their father got ready to leap to Angela's defence if Diabola should try to hit her. But nothing happened. Diabola just stood stock-still. The angry colour left her face and she looked at the ground. Then something extraordinary happened.

She took Angela's hand.

A lightning signal passed between the parents. It was an "attract" time, just when they needed it – a miracle! They walked, on tiptoe as if on glass, to the classroom. The twins walked between them hand-in-hand, just like ordinary children on their first day at school.

The teacher, a nice young woman called Ms Applebough, welcomed them smilingly and showed them to a table with some little chairs round it. They sat down together in silence, still holding hands.

"I can see they're going to settle in straight away," said Ms Applebough warmly to the twins' parents. "You need not stay."

The parents looked at each other. They opened their mouths to say something to Ms Applebough, but they closed them again. Then they did something Ms Applebough thought decidedly odd. They both bent and kissed the pretty little girl. They did not kiss the – (oh dear, what was that word that had nearly surfaced? It couldn't have been "ugly", could it?) – other one.

Ms Applebough thought that was quite wrong. Poor little not-pretty one, how must she feel when her parents kissed her sister and not her? Ms Applebough frowned.

But the parents just turned and walked away. *They* were holding hands, too, the teacher noticed. That was nice. But it wasn't nice for mums and dads to have favourites.

She determined then and there that she would make it up, as much as she could, to little—

"What's your name, sweetie-pie?" she asked Diabola.

Diabola glared at her. Ms Applebough was startled, but she refused to be put off.

"I bet you've got a lovely name, haven't you?"

Diabola said distinctly and dangerously, "Ob damn wib poogle knickers oggsnot."

"Pardon?" said Ms Applebough after a moment.

"Ob—"

"Her name is Dybo," put in Angela hastily. "Mine's Angela."

"Can Dybo talk – er – properly?" asked Ms Applebough.

"She talks to me. I'll tell you what she says."

"OB DAMN WIB POOGLE—"

Angela gave her sister's hand a big squeeze. Dybo squeezed back and Angela fell under the table. She held her squeezed hand in her other hand and bit back her tears.

"Dybo!" said Ms Applebough, shocked. "Did you hurt Angela? You mustn't hurt people, must you?"

Angela scrambled up.

"It's all right," she said bravely. "It didn't hurt. When will the lesson start, please?"

Her blue, heavenly eyes met Ms Applebough's, and something happened in the teacher's heart. No wonder the child's parents had kissed her – Ms Applebough wanted to kiss her. She wanted to take her home with her.

"Now, darling! Right this minute!" she cried. And she raced up to the front of the class, which was now full of little new children sitting round the tables. Some of them were crying and some of them were talking and some of them were just sitting looking worried. Only Angela sat beaming with happiness as Ms Applebough began the first lesson. And only Diabola sat with her hands out of sight, stealthily sawing through the nearest table-leg with a saw-edged knife she'd brought to school with her, and once in a while pinching Angela with her free hand.

There was no trouble until break-time, if you don't count the table falling over. Ms Applebough got a shock, but she was relieved nobody was hurt and called the caretaker to fix it.

When Ms Applebough dismissed the children for break, Angela and Diabola went out into the playground with the others. Angela held Diabola's hand and talked to her in Twinnish.

In the playground they stood off by themselves while the other children ran about, shouted joyfully and played games. Angela watched them wistfully. She would have loved to join in, but she had to stay with Diabola.

The following dialogue took place in Twinnish.

"I wish we could go and play with the others, Dybo."

"No. Stupid, silly others. Won't play."

"Can I go by myself?"

"No. If you do, I'll scream. I'll spit. I'll hit them. I'll throw up!"

Angela stayed.

9. Gym and Other Lessons

Break-time ended. The next lesson was gym.

The gym was rather a large, alarming place to both twins. It echoed and had strange appliances on the walls. Even Angela didn't feel comfortable in it; but it was part of school, so she was determined to be brave and do what was asked of her.

Behind her, Diabola stopped. She stood blocking the doorway and hissed loudly like a snake.

Those who had not already entered the gym tried to push past her. But she held the door-frame and they couldn't.

The gym teacher, a brawny woman called Miss Mursles, strode up to her and said heartily, "Come along then, Corky, time to change."

Diabola looked at her unbelievingly. Change? *Corky*? Her green eyes flashed dangerously and she opened her mouth wide.

Angela rushed over. "She doesn't want to change!" she said quickly. "She wants to stay the same!"

Miss Mursles let out a booming laugh. "Silly

girl! I mean, change her *clothes*. Hurry up now, children, everything off but your vests and gym-knickers."

Diabola released her hold slowly and the other children rushed into the room and began to change. Angela did the same. She folded every garment she took off, and made a neat little squared-off pile. She lined her shoes up. Just as she was ready, she heard another hiss and turned around quickly.

But it was Miss Mursles hissing this time.

She was gazing upward. Angela followed her eyes, and froze.

High on the climbing bars that were fixed to one wall was Diabola. Her clothes and shoes lay scattered about the floor. All her clothes, including her vest and gym-knickers. Including her non-gym knickers.

All the other children gathered round and began to giggle and point.

"Now then, Corky!" called Miss Mursles when she had stopped hissing with shock. "That's quite enough of that! Come down here!"

Diabola responded by spitting neatly in her eye.

Miss Mursles wiped it with one finger. Angela saw her jaw working as she tried to keep her temper.

"She—" Angela began. Miss Mursles turned to

her slowly.

"Are you something to do with that child?" she asked grimly.

Angela explained, and then added, with her usual sweetness, "She doesn't like you calling her Corky. Her name's Dybo."

"Thank. You," said Miss Mursles, very deliberately. She turned back to the climbing bars. "Dybo!" she called up, in a tone that silenced every sniggerer in the room. "Young ladies do not take their clothes off in public. Young ladies do not spit at people."

Diabola proved at once that she was not a young lady.

Miss Mursles wiped her eye again and lost control.

"*Dybo*!" she shouted. "If you are not down from there by the time I count five, I am coming up to get you!"

Angela closed her eyes.

"Miss—" she whispered, but Miss Mursles didn't hear.

"One. Two. Three. Four." She paused. "FIVE!" she finished like a gunshot.

Diabola laughed, stuck her tongue out and replied, "Flurkle-blob natspee!"

Miss Mursles wasted no more time. She took a deep breath and swarmed up the bars like a large monkey. The children below watched with fascination. All except Angela. She couldn't bear to watch, because she knew exactly what would happen next.

And it did.

A few seconds later, there was a cry and a crash. Angela opened her eyes, to see Miss Mursles at the bottom of the bars again in a heap.

Angela rushed forward to help her up.

Miss Mursles seemed dazed.

"She socked me on the jaw," she said. "I didn't even see it coming!"

"I'm sorry," cried Angela. And then, out of her confusion, she heard herself babbling, "She didn't mean to! She doesn't mean to do bad things!"

"So why does she?" asked the teacher, rubbing her jaw and her rear.

"Because... because... because..." Angela's voice rose. "Because I make her!"

Miss Mursles stared at her with her bruised jaw dropped.

"You – make her?"

"Yes! I – make – her – do – bad – things!"

There was an unbelieving silence in the room. Nobody present could believe that this was not a great, big, whopping lie. Even the children already knew by instinct that Angela was good and that Diabola was not. What they didn't know was that this lie was not only great, big and whopping. It was the first and only lie Angela had ever told.

And not one of them knew what Angela was feeling about that, inside. Miss Mursles, who was staring at her, noticed her go very white and sway on her feet, but she didn't know why, and her jaw and her rear – not to mention her pride – hurt too much for her to bother.

"In that case," she said coldly, "you'd better go up there and make her do a good thing. Like coming down and putting some clothes on."

Angela climbed slowly up the bars. Diabola

crouched at the top, hanging on with one hand. The other was free, and swinging dangerously, and so was one foot.

"Don't dare touch me, or you'll get it like she did," she said in Twinnish.

Angela stopped climbing, just out of reach, and said, also in Twinnish, "Did you hear me tell that lie?"

Diabola didn't answer. She just scowled.

"I said you were good and I was bad," Angela went on. "If you don't come down, I'll make them think I'm the bad one. I'll make them think you're good."

Now it was Diabola's turn to go pale.

"You couldn't."

Angela said faintly, "I *can* make them believe I make you do bad things."

Diabola sagged on the bars. She turned her back to the gym and climbed down slowly.

For the moment, Angela had won. But at a terrible cost. A lie was all but impossible for Angela, but she'd managed to tell one, in a good cause.

The last lesson was back in their classroom. Ms Applebough was waiting.

"Now!" she said brightly. "We're going to draw lovely pictures. Won't that be fun?"

Most of the children chorused, "Yes!" Angela, feeling better, cried, "Lovely!" Diabola shouted one word. "Blurk!"

This was a very bad word in Twinnish and Angela nudged her and said, "Shhh!"

"Dob spit iggle 'shhh'!" retorted Diabola. "Blurk stink drains pictiks YUCK!"

"What's the matter?" asked Ms Applebough, looking harassed. "Doesn't Dybo want to draw pictures?"

"Yes," said Angela, looking worried. "She's a very good drawer."

"We say 'artist'," said Ms Applebough, giving out sheets of white paper and lots of crayons. "Well! Let's see how many of us are artists, shall we? You can draw anything you like."

Diabola instantly snatched up all the crayons on her table and swept them into her lap. Other children began to complain.

"Dybo dear," said the teacher, "they're not all for you, you know. Come along, give some of them back."

Dybo gave her a look that stopped her in her tracks.

"Oh," she said. "All right then. Just for now…
Come over here, you others, and I'll give you
some more. I hope you do a really nice picture
with those, Dybo," she said over her shoulder.

"Sput-slurp-snurgle," replied Diabola under
her breath. But she wasn't bothering about Ms
Applebough much. She was too busy drawing.

Soon all the children were equally busy,
including Angela. Angela had brought some
crayons with her. Now she drew a picture of a
scene in Japan. She drew a pagoda, flowering
trees, ladies in kimonos with sun-shades, a man
in a top-knot and wide trousers making a bow.
Then, to show Japan is mainly islands, she drew
some blue sea with a dolphin jumping out of it.
She forgot all about Dybo, who was working
next to her.

Ms Applebough was moving round the
classroom, saying things like "Lovely,
sweetheart, lovely! Is that Mummy? Would you
like to give her some legs? Oh! What a lovely
aeroplane! Is it dropping a nice bomb? Lovely!"
Finally she got around to the table now
occupied only by the twins.

She stopped and looked at Angela's scene. It
was done in lots of colours and was really very
nice. Ms Applebough thought it was a good
excuse to give this adorable child a hug.

"Brilliant, Angela! Super!" she cried. "And

you've labelled everything, too! You *are* a clever girl!" Then she turned to Diabola's picture.

A gasp broke from her lips.

The most horrendous picture lay before her. It showed a big wooden chair with a man in it. He had straps on his arms and legs. On his head he wore a sort of cap with string-like things coming out of it. The man's face wore a very unhappy expression. Diabola was busy drawing in zigzag lines like lightning flashes coming out of him.

"Dybo!" Ms Applebough cried. "Whatever is that?"

Diabola ignored her. She put the finishing touches to the zigzags, and then took a plain pencil from her lap and wrote underneath the picture,

"Deth in ther lekik cher".

Angela glanced over at her sister's picture.

She hid her face in her hands.

Ms Applebough had to fight down the urge to do the same thing. The picture was dreadful. It was quite outside Ms Applebough's experience. She simply didn't know what to do.

Finally she heard herself say, in a croaking voice, the most ridiculous thing.

"The spelling's wrong, dear."

After a moment, Diabola handed her the pencil and said something quite quietly in Twinnish to Angela.

"She says you write it," Angela whispered from behind her hands. "She says, you write it right."

And Ms Applebough, feeling completely helpless, could not stop herself from bending over and writing under Diabola's picture the words: Death in the Electric Chair.

Then she picked up the picture, and, with a strangled sound, ran from the room.

10. The Cuthbertson–Joneses Get a Surprise

Mr and Mrs Cuthbertson-Jones waited on tenterhooks all day for the expected phone-call from the school, demanding that they come at once and take Diabola away. It didn't come.

So shortly before four o'clock they set off together to go and collect the girls.

On the way, they tried to decide what had happened. Something must have, that was all they knew.

"Perhaps Diabola ran away or has been unconscious all day," suggested Mr Cuthbertson-Jones.

Neither of them could think of a single other reason why the expected phone-call had not come. As they got nearer to the school, their footsteps became slower. They felt sure something dreadful was awaiting them.

And indeed, when they cautiously pushed open the reinforced glass door into the school front hall, the first person they saw was a formidable-looking woman whom they both guessed at once must be the headmistress. She was obviously waiting for them.

They both stopped in their tracks. Mrs Cuthbertson-Jones shut her eyes tight as if expecting a blow.

But the headmistress merely came to greet them, shook them each by the hand and said, "Mr and Mrs Cuthbertson-Jones? I am Mrs Kirkbright, the principal of the school. Would you please follow me?"

With dread in their hearts, they did so. She led them into her office and asked them to take a seat.

"Mr and Mrs Cuthbertson-Jones," she began. "I must have a word with you about your daughter Dybo."

They hung their heads. Here it came, without a doubt. She was to be expelled on the spot.

"Our school," said Mrs Kirkbright, "prides itself on being able to look after the needs of all types of children. Bright ones, less able ones, well-adjusted ones, disturbed ones. I might even be old-fashioned and say—" she smiled a tight little smile, "—good ones and naughty ones. I mention this because I don't want there to be any misunderstanding about what I am about to say."

"Oh, there won't be," murmured Mrs Cuthbertson-Jones sadly.

"I'm afraid there was a little *contretemps* with Dybo in the classroom today," she went on. But she didn't sound stern. She sounded coy. "Ms Applebough is, for her age, a very experienced teacher. But even she had never known anything like what occurred."

"No, I would think not," said Mr Cuthbertson-Jones, bracing himself.

"She came straight to me. She was quite distressed. The fact is, she was unable to deal with the situation. It was up to me to judge the seriousness – the momentousness – of what Dybo had done."

Mrs Cuthbertson-Jones swallowed. "What… what had she done?" she asked fearfully.

"This."

Mrs Kirkbright, with a flourish, handed them Diabola's drawing.

Mr Cuthbertson-Jones, bewildered, took it and looked at it. His wife looked too, over his shoulder. They both stared at it aghast, almost unable to believe what they saw.

But nothing in the picture or in their lives

prepared them for Mrs Kirkbright's next words.

"I would like to congratulate you."

Her two listeners raised their heads and stared at her.

"Natural, in-born talent is one thing. But it is very greatly to your credit to have brought her along as you have. You must have a very highly cultured home, and you must devote many many hours to being with Dybo, stimulating and encouraging her. Her achievements are quite extraordinary."

She beamed at the parents.

"You see, Ms Applebough did not realise what she was looking at. Her field is not art. Mine is — or was, till my promotion to headmistress. I am able to recognise genius when I see it."

"Pardon?" asked Mr Cuthbertson-Jones after a stunned moment.

"Oh, yes. Nothing less than genius. Look. Just look at her drawing."

She stood up and came round her desk until she stood beside them, pointing.

"Do you know how most children of her age draw

figures? I assure you it is not like this! Her grasp of anatomy – look at that hand, gripping the arm of the chair! The expression on the face – a most realistic impression of sheer agony! Ah, if this is achieved in the dry wood of infancy, what shall be done in the green wood of maturity!" She clasped her hands in ecstasy. "I myself shall teach her! What a privilege!"

"But – but – but – the subject..." stammered the father.

"The subject? Precisely! The power, the drama!"

"Where did she get such an idea from?" whispered Mrs Cuthbertson-Jones in dismay.

"Where else but at home?" Mrs Kirkbright cried, with every sign of approval. "How splendid that you do not censor her viewing and reading, but let her imagination feed on all the stimulating horrors of our everyday world! Genius must not be censored or held back. And it will not be – not in my school!"

"The – writing..." began Mrs Cuthbertson-Jones in a croaky voice.

"Ah, that is another thing! I am delighted, and deeply impressed, with Dybo's advanced level of spelling."

"'Deth in ther lekik cher' – advanced?"

"It is what we progressive educators call creative spelling," said Mrs Kirkbright. "Far to be preferred to anything conventional. My dear Mr and Mrs Cuthbertson-Jones, I repeat: I congratulate you. You have done splendidly. And now it is for our school to take in hand this budding flower, and make sure it opens for the benefit of the world!"

She returned to her seat and sat down, beaming at them.

There was a stunned silence, and then Mrs Cuthbertson-Jones said faintly, "And Angela. Is she a genius, too?"

The beam faded from Mrs Kirkbright's face.

"Ah. Angela. Well, no, Angela is not of the same extraordinary calibre." She picked up another drawing from her desk. "Here is her artwork." She almost tossed it across to them. "As you see, quite a commonplace bit of work, though I must say, she colours neatly."

"But – but she's labelled everything," said Mr Cuthbertson-Jones. "*She* can write, too!" He exchanged amazed looks with his wife.

"And her spelling is quite right," mentioned Mrs Cuthbertson-Jones timidly. "Pagoda, sunshade, dolphin... Surely that's – rather clever?"

Mrs Kirkbright had lost her sparkle and stifled a yawn. "Quite unremarkable. Quite conventional. We shall have to try to introduce a little more impulsiveness into her work, a little more — how shall I express it? — originality. We must try to see if some of Dybo's brilliance cannot rub off on Angela. But I fear," she said kindly, "that Angela will always be in her sister's shadow."

11. Mr Cuthbertson–Jones Does an Awful Thing

Of course, things changed after that.

They had to. They would have done, probably, in any case, because Mr and Mrs Cuthbertson-Jones had a deep, almost awed respect for Culture, and allowed themselves to think that perhaps their daughter had been put into the world to be a genius and to add to the world's great works of art.

The fact that they thought her drawings were frightening and horrible was not the point, for them. They thought many modern works of art were frightening and horrible, so they assumed that was the proper thing in art nowadays.

For a short while, it seemed to the Cuthbertson-Joneses that the worst of their troubles might be over.

Diabola had never let anyone see what she was drawing and would scrumple up the pages viciously if her parents or sister came near.

But now she drew properly. She drew nearly all the time she was at home. She began early in the morning and continued as soon as she came home from school, until bedtime.

By then she was so tired she gave no trouble. She had no spare energy to do awful things. She ate; she slept; she drew. *What* she drew was appalling, horrendous, disgusting, revolting, and also quite nasty. But it kept her fully occupied, and the Cuthbertson-Joneses' lives became several degrees less ghastly.

She still didn't talk to them, however, which is why they were not prepared for what happened some months later.

Mrs Cuthbertson-Jones came to collect the twins after school and found Mrs Kirkbright waiting. She positively cooed: "Dear Dybo is doing sooooo well! I am thrilled with her progress! And she is thrilled, too. She said so."

Mrs Cuthbertson-Jones stared with her mouth slightly open.

"She talks to you?"

"Of course."

"How?"

"What can you mean? In the normal way."

"But Dybo never speaks in English."

"Is she polyglot?" asked the headmistress eagerly.

"Pardon?"

"Does-she-speak-more-than-one-language?" asked the headmistress with rather overdone patience. "Because she certainly speaks English beautifully to me. She has a very – er – rich vocabulary.

Mrs Cuthbertson-Jones felt stunned. At last she managed to say, "Please tell me exactly what she said. About being thrilled."

"Let me see," said Mrs Kirkbright brightly. "I think her exact words were, 'Isn't this bleeding brilliant?'" She beamed.

"Do you allow her to speak to you like that?" Mrs Cuthbertson-Jones asked timidly. She was almost more shocked at what Diabola had said, than that she had spoken at all.

"Oh, yes!" replied Mrs Kirkbright blithely. "She must be unrestrained. One may not hold back genius!"

"But she shouldn't swear."

"I don't think 'bleeding' was a swear-word in this case. She was describing her drawing."

"What was it?"

"One of her battle scenes," said Mrs Kirkbright casually. "Strewn with corpses. Lots of blood. Chopped-off heads. Highly realistic. Would you care to see it?"

"No thank you," said Mrs Cuthbertson-Jones hastily. "Can't you persuade her to draw something nice?"

"Nice," mused Mrs Kirkbright. "Nice... Such a wishy-washy word. I really don't think that is a word I would associate with Dybo." She laughed indulgently.

Mrs Cuthbertson-Jones could only nod.

She reported this conversation to her husband. They simply didn't know what to make of it. They didn't know what was happening altogether.

Because, although things were different, and, in a way, better, both Diabola's parents worried secretly. She wasn't being so bad any more. Where was all that badness going? Could it be that it was all going into her pictures? Or was it – was it being *stored up* in some way?

They consulted Angela when they were alone with her. Not that it helped much. Angela had a way of avoiding questions she couldn't answer.

"Do you know Dybo *talks* to Mrs Kirkbright?"

"No."

"Does she talk to Ms Applebough?"

"She doesn't like ordinary lessons. She just likes Art."

"How does she behave in class?"

"She doesn't behave."

They looked at each other.

"She doesn't behave? How do you mean, darling?"

Angela looked anxious but didn't reply.

Though at first they didn't know what Angela

meant by "She doesn't behave", watching Diabola, they began to understand. Diabola didn't behave badly. She didn't behave well. She didn't *behave* at all. In some curious way, she just *was*.

She no longer screamed, kicked, spat and threw things, unless, of course, someone annoyed her. By now, her parents and sister knew what would be likely to annoy her, and so they avoided doing it, as far as they could.

The morning routine now went something like this. Mrs Cuthbertson-Jones would come into the twins' room and open the curtains. Then she would go to Angela's bed and wake her with a kiss. They would sometimes have a little chat, in very low whispers. Then Mrs Cuthbertson-Jones would go to Diabola's cage.

When she raised the curtain-thing, instead of finding Diabola standing behind the bars, glaring, she would be lying on the floor. Drawing.

The chief difficulty was to persuade her to stop drawing long enough to get ready for school. She dressed herself, but washing was a serious problem. Diabola had no desire to be clean, and had never brushed her teeth in her life. Her parents had long ago given up trying to get her to wash, as such. Fortunately she liked lying in very hot water, and gnawing on hard foods like bones, so she was not as unfresh or unhealthy as she might have been.

She no longer had to be dragged to school. On the contrary. She would put her papers and pencils, crayons and paintbox into her schoolbag and leave the house as soon as she'd stuffed some food into her mouth. (Her table-manners were too revolting to describe.)

Her father had to be ready to go with her because now she could open the front door (when they'd fitted a top bolt to keep her in, she had whacked the inside of the door with a chair), she would simply set off for school as soon as she wanted to go.

Sometimes, on the way, Mr Cuthbertson-Jones would remember earlier days when he had talked to Diabola and she would scream, "Toopid Daddy TALK a-Dybo NOW!" in understandable English. It was so long since she had addressed him directly that even that not-very-pleasant memory made him wistful.

So he would talk to her on the way to school. Little remarks such as, "I'm so glad you like your drawing lesson, Diabola. Mrs Kirkbright says you're doing very well." Or: "Look at the birdie, it's singing for the spring!" Mr Cuthbertson-Jones was still trying to act as if Diabola were a perfectly normal child. Being perfectly normal himself, he knew no other way.

But Diabola would stare straight ahead as if she didn't even notice he was there, never mind listening to him.

One day, however, as they were walking along, and Mr Cuthbertson-Jones was making these mild, wistful remarks, he happened to say something that annoyed Diabola. All it was, was something like, "You're looking so much nicer now you've let Mummy cut an inch off your corkscrews." (Of course Diabola had never in her life allowed anyone to brush or comb her hair, so her corkscrews had become matted and tended to get full of dust and small living things such as earwigs and moths.)

Diabola was walking ahead as usual, and her father saw her stop dead. He had to stop dead too, not to bump into her. In fact he stepped back a little. So he had a good view of Diabola as she turned slowly around.

She dropped her schoolbag on the pavement and made the most grotesque face he had ever seen. She put her thumbs in her mouth and pulled it wide. She crossed her eyes and pulled her lower eyelids down with her middle fingers, showing the red. She stuck her little fingers up her nose. Then she thrust her tongue out as far as it would go and made a really gross noise with it.

A woman who was passing said, "Tsk-tsk! Disgusting!" But worse for Mr Cuthbertson-Jones was a man who smirked at him and said, "That's putting you in your place, mate!"

Something inside him – something kind, patient and long-suffering – seemed to snap.

"I'm going to stop talking to you, Diabola. I don't think I'll ever talk to you again."

Diabola had already stopped making her face and begun to walk on. But when he said these words, she stopped, and her back went stiff. Now he knew for certain that she had heard every kind word he had ever spoken to her and was just ignoring him out of spite.

And suddenly he was so very angry and hurt that he did an awful thing. He shouted, "And you can go to school on your own!", turned on his heel, and left her there.

He walked home without once looking back. In his head was seething a most dreadful thought: "I don't care what happens to her! I don't care if I never see her again!"

He was just turning in at his front gate, and his anger had begun to give way to guilt, when something hit him hard in the seat of his trousers.

He whirled round.

Behind him was Diabola. She was backing off, getting ready to land another kick.

He stared at her. She was purple in the face with rage, and when she saw he couldn't be kicked in the pants again, she prepared to kick him in the shins.

But his blood was up. As she ran at him and

swung her leg, he caught her foot in one hand.

She fell on her bottom.

Her father swiftly picked up her other foot, and lifted her until she hung upside-down. Then he threw her over his shoulder and carried her bodily into the house, ignoring her efforts to hit him with her fists.

He marched straight into the twins' bedroom and thrust Diabola into the cage, locked it, and pulled down the curtain. He heard a crash as she hurled herself against the bars, and then a stream of abuse in Twinnish. But he ignored it.

As soon as she drew breath, he said, quite calmly considering how his heart was thumping, "You will have to stay there all day, Diabola, and not go to school. In fact," he went on after the screech that followed, "you won't go to school again at all unless you show me you're sorry for kicking me."

He waited for the next screech, but it didn't come. He turned to leave the room. Suddenly he stopped, electrified.

Diabola's voice came from behind the curtain, muffled but perfectly clear.

"You left me. I kicked you because you left me."

He slowly turned and went back a few steps.

"Say that again, Diabola."

She did.

He pulled up the curtain and they stared at one another.

"I left you," he said, "because I am sick and tired of talking to you and being nice to you and having you treat me as if I were nothing."

Diabola's green eyes were narrowed to slits. This was a very bad sign. Her father had learnt to back down (and back away) quickly when this happened, but now he stood his ground.

She said, "You are nothing."

He felt this much more than when she'd kicked him. But he didn't show it.

"If I'm nothing," he said between his teeth, "why did you mind that I left you?"

"You're my Daddy. You have to take me to school."

"Have to? I don't have to."

"Yes you DO. I'm little. Someone could hurt me."

He almost laughed. "Hurt you, Diabola? I don't think so. The other way around, perhaps."

"You or Mummy always take Pigface to school."

"Are you talking about your sister?"

"Pigface."

"*Angela* deserves to be taken to school and loved and looked after. If anything happened to *Angela*, we'd care."

When he heard these terrible words come out of his mouth, Mr Cuthbertson-Jones had a sense of horror. He turned and ran out of the room.

His wife had by now left to walk Angela to school. He waited for her to come back, feeling worse and worse every moment. He sat by the kitchen table and hid his face in his hands.

He'd long suspected he was not a very good man. But was he as bad as this? Was he this dreadful person – this sinner? No one who wasn't could have said such a thing to his child, never mind leaving her alone in the street.

What was happening to him? He had tried so hard to love her, or at least to treat her properly and be fair to her. She was turning him into a monster!

When he heard his wife shutting the front door, he got up and went to meet her. She took one look at his face and gave a cry.

"My dear! What's happened?"

"She spoke to me."

"She spoke?"

"Yes, and I wish she hadn't. She said terrible things. I said terrible things. I hate myself. I'm sorry, dear, but I don't think I can carry on."

And, for the first time, Mr Cuthbertson-Jones broke down in tears.

12. Mr Cuthbertson–Jones Does Something Even Worse

At about eight o'clock a few mornings later, Angela was lying in bed listening to the birds singing and sensing Dybo beyond the curtain. She felt happy and content because things were right in her world, so far as she knew.

But after about half an hour she grew worried.

"If Mummy doesn't come to wake me up soon, I'm going to be late for school!" she thought.

It occurred to her that she was already awake, and that perhaps her parents were not. She got up and went into her parents' little room, which had been the twins' when they were babies.

It was only just wide enough for a double bed, so Mr and Mrs Cuthbertson-Jones had to get in and out of it from the bottom.

Angela's mother was sitting on the bottom of the bed in her nightgown, with her feet dangling. She had a piece of paper in her hand.

"Mummy. Is something wrong?" asked Angela in her sweet little voice.

Her mother looked up at her. Angela saw at

once that something was very wrong indeed and she felt fear in her heart.

"Mummy?"

But her mother didn't – couldn't – answer.

Angela crept closer to her mother.

"Who's that letter from?" she asked in a trembly voice.

Her mother whispered, "It's from Daddy."

"What does it say?"

"He's gone," Mrs Cuthbertson-Jones replied in hollow tones.

Angela took the paper from her mother and looked at it. She read very well for her age but the letter was in joined-up writing and was too hard for her. But she could make out the word "Dear" at the top, and "sorry" at the bottom.

Angela dropped the paper and put both arms round her mother. But for once her mother didn't respond. She just sat there very stiffly on the end of the bed with her hands clenched in her lap.

Then they both heard a familiar sound: the crash as Diabola, across the corridor, hurled herself at the bars of the cage, her signal that she wanted to get out.

A long shudder passed through Mrs Cuthbertson-Jones' slender frame. Then she stood up, put Angela aside and walked in her nightdress and bare feet from the room.

She entered the twins' room and pulled up the

curtain-thing with a jerk. Angela watched from the doorway. Her heart was beating very fast. She felt instinctively that whatever happened now, would change things yet again.

Mrs Cuthbertson-Jones was by nature a meek, quiet woman. It was her firm belief that a woman should always be calm and gentle, look after things in the home and do her best to please her family. She very seldom lost her temper.

Diabola stood before her, enraged that schooltime was near and that no one had come to release her. Her little green eyes were slitty, her hands, gripping the bars, had white knuckles, and she was shaking with fury.

On any normal morning, had Diabola shown such dangerous signs, her mother would at once have called her husband and asked him to stand by her when she opened the cage. But he was gone. Now there was no one to help Mrs Cuthbertson-Jones except Angela.

Mrs Cuthbertson-Jones reached behind her and beckoned Angela to her side. They could both hear Diabola's teeth chattering with rage. Angela could sense her mother trembling.

Mrs Cuthbertson-Jones took Angela by the hand, then straightened and braced herself. She'd had a lot of practice bracing herself, and she did it quite well. Holding Angela's hand suddenly made her even better at it.

"Jane," she said.

Her voice sounded different. It was firm and quite loud, not the rather fluttery little voice they were used to.

Diabola opened her slitty eyes wide.

She turned to her sister, and asked her one short question in Twinnish.

"Chunk piddle 'Jane'?"

"Tell her," their mother said, before Angela could even translate, "that Jane is her. It's her name from now on. Actually, don't bother, she understands perfectly." She stepped boldly up to the bars and crouched down till her face was level with Diabola's. This was highly unwise, but she did it, and oddly, nothing happened.

"I know you can talk, Jane. Now if you want to go to school or have a bath or eat or do anything, you will have to talk to me. That includes drawing. No more drawing unless you talk."

This last – about the drawing – was what caused Diabola's face to grow pale and her hands to clench more strongly on the bars. But there was no relenting in her expression, which grew fiercer and more defiant than ever.

"Chongle erpburp slurch sniggle sickbag," she said slowly and menacingly.

Her mother glanced at Angela, who said faintly, "She says she'll pee on the floor."

This gave Mrs Cuthbertson-Jones pause, but only for a moment. She couldn't let herself back down for a bit of pee.

"That's up to her," she said. "You can move into my room, Angela."

"Slapcrap snurgle blurk!" shouted Diabola. "Upchuck tungout gungedroppings!"

"She says she's got enough drawing paper in the cage and you can't stop her drawing."

"Spitball gutsnuggle willy slimebag," continued Diabola distinctly.

"She says if you don't give her food she'll die and you'll go back to prison," said Angela.

As she said the word "prison", Angela burst into tears. She detached herself from her mother, threw herself down near the cage, reached her arms in and tried to take hold of Diabola's ankles. Diabola stepped back, out of her reach. Angela began to plead and beg. Diabola kicked at her and tried to tread on her fingers. Angela withdrew her arms and clutched her mother's ankles instead.

"Mummy, Mummy, please don't let her die!"

"Nonsense, she's not going to die," said Mrs Cuthbertson-Jones with unusual firmness. "As to having plenty of paper to draw on, I shall have to attend to that."

She reached for the padlock.

Angela stopped crying and jumped to her feet.

"Mummy! Don't go in!"

But Mrs Cuthbertson-Jones didn't listen. She undid the padlock, opened the gate of the cage, went inside, and very quickly padlocked the gate from inside and threw the key through the bars to the outside.

By this time Diabola was upon her.

She was like a wild thing. She pummelled and scratched and kicked and even tried to bite.

Mrs Cuthbertson-Jones was not used to dealing with Diabola on this level. When it was necessary to subdue her by force, she had sometimes helped her husband, but she had never done it by herself. She'd never had to.

114

Now, in her moment of despair, knowing that she was alone and abandoned, an extraordinary strength came to her, strength she'd never known she had.

She seized Diabola by both wrists, held them together, pushed her away, and stood her back on her feet. Then she hooked one foot round Diabola's ankles, pushed her over, and lay on her. Diabola struggled wildly but she couldn't free her hands. Inch by inch Mrs Cuthbertson-Jones shifted both of them across the few feet of the floor to the pile of paper and crayons that lay in the corner where Diabola normally drew.

Mrs Cuthbertson-Jones levered herself up onto her knees, holding Diabola on her back on the floor. She put one knee on Diabola's legs so she couldn't kick. Then with her free hand, she began to crumple the paper page by page and throw it out through the bars. Some of the paper balls hit the bars and bounced back, but anyway they were no more use for drawing on.

Diabola went absolutely crazy. She twisted and writhed and seethed and frothed and flung herself about. She tried her utmost to free herself, but Mrs Cuthbertson-Jones hung on grimly until every last page had been crumpled.

Then, still holding Diabola's wrists, she stood up, lifting the struggling Diabola up too.

"I'm going to let go now, Jane," she said, trying

not to puff. "If you attack me again I'm going to leave you here all day and Angela will never sleep in this room again!"

"No!" cried Angela from outside the cage. "Don't say that, Mummy! I want to sleep here!"

Whenever Angela asked for anything, it was almost impossible for her mother to refuse her. She looked at Angela and said, "Then you tell her not to hurt me."

Angela rushed to the bars, talking rapidly in Twinnish. (Angela's Twinnish didn't sound a bit like Diabola's of course, but Diabola understood it.) What she was actually saying was, "Dybo, don't! Don't fight! Daddy's gone away! If you fight, Mummy might go too, and then we'll be all alone!"

It might, possibly, have saved Mrs Cuthbertson-Jones a lot of effort and some bruises if Angela had told Diabola this in the first place. Whatever threats Diabola might make about dying, she didn't mean them. She had every intention of living a long time, and while she was doing it she wanted to be comfortable, well-fed and looked after. Her father was a big part of that.

It had never occurred to her that she could drive him so far; he had always seemed so strong and patient. When she understood that he had left, she was so surprised, and so frightened, that she at once stopped struggling and sat down on the floor. It was the nearest thing to a faint that she was capable of. She had gone as white as chalk and her body had lost all strength for the moment.

"Angela. Hand me the key."

Angela did so, and Mrs Cuthbertson-Jones lost no time in letting herself out of the cage and locking it behind her. She was almost fainting herself from the stress of the last few minutes, but there was something of triumph, too, in her bearing as she said, "Bring your clothes to my room, Angela. You're going to be late for school if we don't hurry. I'll get your breakfast."

And she strode out.

Angela gave one anguished look at her sister through the bars, then gathered up her school clothes in their neatly squared-off pile and ran after her mother, leaving Diabola-Jane slumped on the floor.

13. Diabola Behaves

A few days later, Angela received her very first letter.

Her mother handed it to her at the breakfast table with the words, "It's from Daddy."

She made no other comment, and she didn't ask what the letter said. She just got on with the breakfast and kept her back turned.

But Dybo did more than ask. She tried to snatch the envelope out of Angela's hand.

Usually when Diabola snatched at something she wanted, Angela at once let go of it. But not this time.

This time she jumped up, holding the letter very tight, and ran into the bedroom with it. Diabola ran after her, hissing and trying to grab her from behind. Angela rushed into the cage and blocked the gate as she had often seen Diabola do, by pushing the bed against it.

Diabola hurled herself against the bars.

"MY cage!" she screamed. "MY bed! Come OUT!"

"My letter," said Angela.

She sat on the bed to add her weight, as

Diabola was now flinging herself against the gate. Angela opened the letter with trembling hands.

It was a single sheet of paper with printed writing. Angela concentrated all her reading skills on it. She was able to read most of it.

Dearest Angela,

I ran away. I am no good to you or Mummy. I am weak and (Here were two long words that Angela couldn't manage.) I have tried with your sister. I can't any more. You can love her because you are good. I can't because I'm bad. She gets it from me. She is my (another long word, beginning with 'p'.) Tell Mummy I am sorry.

Love, Daddy.

At the bottom, he had written: Keep loving me, if you can.

It was these final words that brought tears to Angela's eyes.

Normally, Diabola enjoyed nothing better than to see Angela cry. She would clap her hands with glee, or – a strange habit of hers when excited – she would clutch her bottom with both hands and jump around in circles.

This time, however, she was so infuriated that she rattled the cage door and shrieked: "What's he SAY, Pigface, what's he SAY, is he coming back? TELL ME or you'll be SORRY!"

But Angela couldn't show her the letter. Angela could always imagine how she herself would feel. If she'd been Dybo, the letter would have hurt *her* feelings dreadfully.

She raised her tear-stained, beautiful face.

"He says he's weak and bad," she whispered.

"YES YES YES!" cried Diabola, and now she did clutch her bottom and jump round in circles.

"No! He's good!" Angela tried to say, but Diabola's crowings and jumpings drowned her voice.

"He's BAD! He LEFT! I made him leave!" she screeched.

"But now you want him back."

Diabola heard this and stopped to think about it.

"Yes. To make me safe. Mouldy Mummy can't make me safe."

"Don't you love him?" ventured Angela, tears still streaming.

She should have known better.

Diabola looked at her with her lip curled.

"You make me throw up," she said, and walked out of the room.

But the departure of her father had had a strange effect on Diabola even before the letter came.

Mrs Cuthbertson-Jones had found out what Angela had meant when she'd said Diabola "didn't behave."

Because Diabola had now begun to behave.

Behaving, in Diabola's case, turned out to mean not being herself. It meant putting on an act. Covering her true nature. Behaving.

Even though this made life bearable for Mrs Cuthbertson-Jones, neither she nor Angela felt happy about it. Because, since Diabola didn't know any other way to behave, what she did was to copy Angela.

She did a sort of awful, false imitation of her. She crept around the place with a sickly-sweet smile on her face. She put on a sweet little trilling voice. She certainly talked, but it was mainly to lisp, "Yeth Mummy, no Mummy" all the time.

One of her favourite tricks in the past had been to squeeze out the toothpaste tubes and smear the toothpaste all over the mirror, the taps, the bathmat and the walls. Now, intent on "behaving", she tried to brush her teeth. But she'd never done it before. She sneezed wetly in the middle and splattered toothpaste. Of course this was an accident, which makes it all the stranger that it was for this that she made her very first apology.

She ran to her mother pretending to cry (she did this by saying "Boo-hoo-hoo!" very loudly –

no tears, of course), and trilling, "Thowwy I made a meth, Mummy, don't be cwoth wiv me!"

Mrs Cuthbertson-Jones could only stare at her helplessly.

After meals, instead of hurling dishes to the floor (all dishes in the house were unbreakable), she jumped up, beating Angela to the sink with dirty plates, chirruping, "Thowwy, Angelah!" every time she bumped into her or trod on her foot. She insisted on trying to wash up, another thing she'd never done in her life, and when inevitably she made the floor wet, she turned on such a look of woe and shame that her mother shut her eyes tight, in case the temptation to thump her should become too much for her to control.

Never, ever, had Mrs Cuthbertson-Jones found Diabola so absolutely infuriating as now that she was trying to "behave".

And now Angela began to change.

She went back to babyishness. She pulled her hair down over her eyes and sucked her fingers. She mumbled and curled up in corners. She no longer talked in her ordinary voice. Since Diabola had begun to copy her, Angela seemed to be trying to stop giving her sister anything to copy.

Her mother, who was at her wits' end one way and another, found this the last straw.

She had never had to raise her voice to Angela, of course. But now she did.

"Angela, stop that! I want you to behave!"

Angela burst into tears and crawled behind the sofa.

Her mother screamed: "Come out and stop this nonsense, it's driving me mad!"

Two things then happened at once. Diabola, who had been out in the garden digging a hole for someone to fall into, heard the unbelievable sound of her mother shouting at her sister, and raced into the room, her face alight with excitement. She skidded to a halt practically under her mother's nose.

The other thing that happened was that Angela, shattered by the anger in her mother's voice, emerged from behind the sofa and rushed towards her. The twins collided.

Diabola reverted to her normal manner. She grasped a handful of her sister's hair, pulled it hard, and crowed, "She hates you now!"

"No!" cried Angela in horror.

"YES! Look at her face, she's angry!"

"Please stop pretending to be me, Jane!"

"I like being you! You're so icky! You're so phoney! You're so creepy! And my name's Diabola! You're so stupid you don't even know my name!"

Angela looked at her mother, who was standing there bewildered, not able to understand what they were saying.

"Mummy, why do you call Dybo Jane now?" asked Angela tearfully.

Her mother swallowed, and, as gently as she could in the temper she was in, prised Diabola's fingers loose from Angela's beautiful hair.

"Dybo is short for Diabola. Diabola means 'bad'. Jane is the name I chose for her, the name I wanted to call her. Maybe people act up to their names."

The twins gazed at her, both, in their own way, baffled by this new idea.

"Did you want to call me something different?" Angela asked. If her mother hadn't known her better, she might have thought she detected a tiny tinge of envy in Angela's voice.

She rejected this mad idea (envy was a horrid thing – Angela couldn't be capable of it!). But Diabola had heard it too, and she had no difficulty believing it. Before her mother could answer, she shouted, "You want another name? I'll give you a name! Your name's—" And here she took up a fighting position, and with each word she punched the air and stamped her foot, "Pig-face, Stink-pot, Scum-bag, Slime-ball, Snot-rag, Toe-cheese—"

Mrs Cuthbertson-Jones' hands were suddenly reaching out. She couldn't stop them! They were closing round Diabola's shoulders when a loud cry from Angela stopped her.

"Yes! Yes! I am like that! And your name's Sweet-pea, Cream-pie, Sunshine, Rosebud, Love-heart, Pumpkin—"

The other two stared at her. Instead of shadow-boxing, as Diabola had, to accompany the string of names, Angela, with every tender name, blew a desperate kiss.

Diabola snarled, flung off her mother's suddenly limp hands, and launched herself at Angela like a tigress.

Before their mother could do anything, Diabola had Angela on her back and was banging her head on the floor, screaming frenziedly, "Don't call me nice names! You make me sick, you icky sticky creepy crawlie little goody-goody!"

Mrs Cuthbertson-Jones dragged her off, and carried her towards the cage in the bedroom, while Diabola shrieked back at Angela on the floor, "Don't you dare love me! I hate you! I wish you were dead!"

Angela rolled onto her stomach, put her face in the carpet, and wished so too – until she remembered that it's very wrong to wish to be dead.

Mrs Cuthbertson-Jones locked Diabola up and stood still to recover her breath. Then her eyes met those little glaring green ones, now red-rimmed with fury, and she said, as calmly as she was able, "I don't want you to behave any more, I'd rather you were just you. Now listen: You've done lots and lots of bad things. You've driven your father away. You've made me miserable. Even your sister doesn't love you at the moment. She's only pretending to because that's all she knows. So everything's all wrong. Everything's just terrible. Everything's just the way you want it to be. Isn't it – Diabola?"

Just as she was turning to leave, something strange happened. Diabola shot out her hand and pointed at her. That was all – then. But some time later, when Mrs Cuthbertson-Jones was in the kitchen, she felt a burning, itching sensation on her arm.

She pulled up her sleeve. There was a round, red mark, like a burn.

It took a whole day for the mark to fade.

14. A House Divided

Some days later, the vicar – the same one – happened to be walking past the end of the road where the Cuthbertson-Joneses lived. He saw a commotion going on half-way down so, having nothing better to do, he wandered along to see what was going on.

All sorts of vehicles and people were out in the street, and it wasn't long before he was near enough to see why they were there.

The Cuthbertson-Joneses' house had fallen down.

It had been a small house, joined to other houses on each side. The strange thing was, just their house had collapsed. Very neatly. It had not pulled even one brick out of the houses it was joined to. Their walls were still upright, with just a few bits of cement sticking to them.

The Cuthbertson-Joneses' house was nothing but a heap of rubble.

The vicar remembered only too clearly that house and who lived there. In a flash of guilt, he recalled his terrible failure to expel the badness from the bad child, his refusal even to try to expel the goodness from the angelic one.

Now the house lay in ruins. Only one thing stood up lopsidedly among the rubble. A cage-front. Metal bars, a gate, a padlock. Though the crowd outside was pointing to this with much puzzlement, the vicar, of course, was not puzzled in the least.

Not one other bit of the house was still standing. Apart from all the hubbub in the street, a deathly stillness lay in front of him.

In a blinding flash, the vicar knew what had happened.

In fact, now he thought about it, the only surprise was that the house had not crumbled to dust much sooner.

He should have warned them. Now they were all dead. And he would have this terrible tragedy on his conscience forever.

And yet... And yet...

That that angel-child should be dead brought a sense of anguish and loss to his heart. But when he remembered the eyes of the other one, when he thought that she was gone from the world, a most un-vicarly feeling stirred in his heart. A feeling that he could only call – relief.

At this moment, a policeman came up to him.

"Awful, eh, vicar?" he said in surprisingly cheerful tones.

"Awful," agreed the vicar hollowly.

"What would make a house collapse like that, eh? All at once. Not a brick or slate left whole. Unnatural, somehow."

"Yes," said the vicar. "Unnatural. That's the word." He didn't want to talk. He turned to go.

"Hard to believe anyone survived."

The vicar turned sharply. "What?"

"Unbelievable, eh? Mother must have sensed something. She got one of the little girls out in time."

The vicar grabbed the policeman by the front of his tunic.

"Which one? *Which one?*"

"Steady on, vicar! I dunno which one, do I? Pretty little thing, like an angel—"

"Oh! Thank heaven!" breathed the vicar, letting go and clasping his hands.

"The other one—" began the policeman.

"Crushed to a pulp, no doubt?" the vicar asked, trying not to sound too hopeful.

"No."

"No?"

The policeman shook his head. "The rescue workers went in this morning. Hadn't a hope, of course. Mother – surprisingly calm, she was – showed 'em where to dig. Behind those bars. Funny arrangements some families have, eh? Anyhow, there she was. Under the bed, covered three feet deep with rubble. Fast asleep. Not even scratched."

"Oh, my God," said the vicar under his breath.

"You may well say so, vicar," said the policeman. "Bit of a miracle all right."

A miracle, was it? thought the vicar. But not the heavenly kind!

"And – and the husband?"

The policeman shook his head. "Gone. So I heard. Left. Pushed off. A week ago. Just in time, eh?"

The vicar straightened himself. There was work here for him.

"Where are they now?" he asked in a

strengthened voice.

"Council's got 'em in a hostel," said the policeman, and gave him the address.

Mrs Cuthbertson-Jones was sitting in a chair in the hostel holding a cup of tea with shaking hands. Beside her in two cardboard boxes were the few things the rescue workers had managed to save from the wreck of the house.

Angela was at her side, leaning against her. Her face was pale as paper. This only made her more beautiful and angelic, like a painting by Botticelli.

Diabola was sitting in a corner of the room with her back turned. She was drawing what looked at first glance like a jolly Hallowe'en scene on the wall with wax crayons. There was a kindly-looking middle-aged woman watching her. She didn't try to stop her. She was prepared to allow anything that helped this unfortunate family to get over their ordeal.

The vicar came in quietly and drew a chair up beside Mrs Cuthbertson-Jones.

"My poor dear lady," he said. "What can I say?"

Mrs Cuthbertson-Jones turned and stared at him. She had lost the patient, meek look she had had in the days when he saw her at her husband's side every Sunday in church. He hadn't seen her there for a long time.

"What can you say? You can tell me why it

happened," she said. "Only I'm sure you can't really."

"Oh yes," he said, "I think I can do that."

She put down the cup. "Go on."

"Could we be alone?" he said, glancing at the twins.

Mrs Cuthbertson-Jones looked at him for a moment. Then she glanced at the kindly-looking woman, who nodded brightly. Yes, she would take care of the girls. Mrs Cuthbertson-Jones led the way into the next room and shut the door after them. They both sat down.

"Go on," she said again.

The vicar made a steeple of his fingers.

"A house divided against itself must fall," he said.

"I've heard that," she said. "But what does it mean?"

"I'm speaking of something perfectly rational, something subject to the law of physics."

"Physics?"

He nodded. "The laws of matter. You see, good and evil are not supposed to be divided as they are in the twins. They are supposed to be mixed together in all of us. When they are so mixed, the good checks the bad, the bad modifies the good. I call this balance."

"Yes, yes, but—"

"Please. Bear with me. Now. In your children, the

good and the bad are split. There is no balance. It seems possible to me that the very atoms and molecules around such extremes might react."

She blinked. "You mean, the atoms and molecules that made up our house might just—"

"Break apart. Disintegrate. Precisely."

"But why didn't it happen years ago?"

"Yes. That is a problem, certainly." He sat frowning thoughtfully.

"It couldn't have had anything to do with my husband leaving, could it?"

The vicar sat up straight. "Of course!" he cried. "Of course it could! Balance! Now, when your husband, who I know to be a good man, was present in the house, together with you and Angela, the three of you together might have been enough to balance the wickedness in Diabola."

Mrs Cuthbertson-Jones gave him a startled look.

"Are you saying it took three good people to – balance the bad in Diabola?"

"It's a terrible fact that evil is sometimes a stronger force than good."

"You know what I thought, about the house falling down?"

"What?"

"That Diabola had caused it on purpose."

"With herself inside? I think that's unlikely. She wouldn't want to kill herself."

"So you're sure she – she – she has no – "

"What, dear lady?"

"Supernatural powers?"

They sat staring at each other. The vicar had gone cold.

"Why do you say that?"

"She's been so dreadful lately. Of course she's always been dreadful, but she's got worse. When she was little she once tried to make me put Angela into the drier. And we caught her showing Angela how to poke her finger into an electric socket."

The vicar jumped with dismay. "Good heavens! You mean, she tried to – to kill her?"

"Well, yes! Yesterday I caught her rigging up a booby-trap in our apple tree. You know, the kind where a noose drops round your neck and swings you—"

"This is worse than I thought! How can a little girl – even a bad one—"

"And that's another thing. She's – she's not like a little girl. She's getting less like a little girl every day."

"Well, but – supernatural—?"

"Once we had a struggle. Afterwards she pointed her finger at me. There was a strange mark… Could she make that happen? Oh, vicar! Is this all my fault? I know my husband thinks it's his!"

The vicar passed his hand across his brow. This was getting too much for him. He understood very well why Mr Cuthbertson-Jones had run away. It was a wonder he hadn't done it earlier.

The vicar laid his hand on Mrs Cuthbertson-Jones' shoulder.

"Poor lady. You are not to blame for these children! Some terrible cosmic accident happened before they were born."

"Vicar, you're very kind and comforting."

"I've been useless. I've been a coward and a failure. But I want to help you now."

"Oh, if only you could! I need help so badly!"

At this moment a sense of someone watching them made both turn towards the door. Angela was standing there with an anxious look on her face.

"What is it, Angela?"

"Mummy, the nursey lady has run away."

They hurried next door. And stopped.

The wall Diabola had been working on was now covered with a terrifying scene. The witches, goblins and ghosts she had been drawing before, and which at first glance had looked quite playful, had lost all likeness to a Hallowe'en cartoon. With a few extra touches of the crayon, she had transformed them into things of horror.

Their eyes were glaring with malice, their hands reached out menacingly, their faces were contorted. One could almost hear them cackling and screeching through their twisted mouths.

It was a scene from hell.

15. A New Home

The vicar was all but struck dumb by Diabola's wall-picture. But what struck him was not just its horribleness, but its accomplishment. He could hardly believe that a child not yet seven years old could draw so well.

Diabola was now standing on a chair, which she had set on a table, and was busy decorating the ceiling of the room with black-cloaked vampires, fiends and other hideous creatures, half-human and half-monster, flying overhead. The vicar noticed dazedly that she was using both hands at once. He had read somewhere that this was a sign of evil power.

Her mother, after a paralysed moment, went up to the table, laid hands on the chair, gave it a shake which caused Diabola to drop her crayons and clutch at its back, and said in a shrill but controlled voice: "What an amazingly horrible picture, Diabola. It's really quite sickening and terrifying. Now come down before you fall down and hurt yourself." And she gave the chair another shake.

Diabola climbed down, her face dark with

anger. She got down on the floor to pick up her crayons. Her mother said levelly, "This is the vicar who gave you the name Diabola. He knows all about you."

Diabola looked up quickly from the floor. She flashed such a look at the vicar that his very soul seemed to shiver.

She got up and came towards him. He longed to turn and run, but he forced himself to stand firm.

Suddenly it wasn't just her awfulness that he saw. In a flash of insight, he realised that there was something else about her that was not child-like.

He knew that this child was not exactly a child. It wasn't just in her drawing that she was far in advance of her age. It wasn't a six-and-a-half-year-old that faced him.

Could her mother have been right? Was there something – uncanny here? Something not of this world?

Before Diabola could speak, the door opened and two people from the council came in.

They stopped dead when they saw the murals. One, a stout middle-aged man, uttered a scream and clapped his hands over his eyes. The woman next to him stiffened herself and gave his arm a bracing pinch.

"Mrs Cuthbertson-Jones? I am Mrs Bashforth."

Instead of shaking hands she pointed at the wall. "Graffiti is not allowed," she said frostily. "Especially not that kind of thing. Someone will have the job of cleaning it off, after you've gone."

"Where are we to go?" asked Mrs Cuthbertson-Jones.

"We have had to put you at the top of the list," said Mrs Bashforth. "Fortunately a flat has fallen vacant. It's not perhaps *quite* what you've been used to, but beggars can't be choosers. You can't stay here. The Matron has made that very clear."

She glanced with disgust at the wall, as if to say she thoroughly appreciated the Matron's point of view.

"If you will follow me, a police car is waiting outside to take you to your new home."

Mrs Cuthbertson-Jones touched the vicar's sleeve. "Please will you come with us?"

The vicar looked into Mrs Cuthbertson-Jones' beseeching eyes, swallowed, and said, "Of course, my dear lady, if you wish."

After his years of cowardly neglect, it was the least he could do.

Angela sat in the police car close to her mother. A policeman in a flat cap sat in front of her and drove the four of them through the streets. Mrs Bashforth was following closely in her own car.

Angela watched the buildings getting taller and dingier as the car drove along. She understood that they were going out of their own district into another one, less leafy and pleasant. She understood more. Their lives were going to change completely, and not, she was afraid, for the better.

She felt her mother trembling and slipped her hand into hers. On her other side she felt Diabola give her a sharp poke in the ribs. It hurt (Diabola had very strong, sharp fingers) but Angela didn't say anything. She just wished Diabola would not poke her again. And she didn't. She, too, was gazing out of the window in alarm.

They passed some tall blocks of flats. They didn't look to Angela like buildings people could have homes in. Surely they weren't going to have to live high up in one of these awful blocks?

But it seemed they were.

The police car drove up outside one block, and so did Mrs Bashforth. They all got out, and in silence Mrs Bashforth led the way up some thickly littered steps, past what might once have been lawns and rose-beds, and into a doorway.

Angela drew back. The hall smelt very bad and had rubbish in its corners. Mrs Bashforth said something that sounded like "Animals!" Angela thought she meant that animals lived here, not people, and wondered what kind. Not anything too big, she hoped.

Mrs Bashforth was pressing a button next to a door. Nothing happened.

"They've broken the lift again!" she exclaimed crossly.

Angela knew what a lift was and thought if the animals were cows or elephants, no wonder they'd broken it.

Mrs Bashforth was leading the way up the stone stairs. It was a very long climb. Long before they got there, the twins began to stumble as their legs grew tired.

Mrs Cuthbertson-Jones picked Angela up, and the policeman, who was still with them, picked up Diabola. Angela shut her eyes tight, expecting something awful to happen, but Diabola didn't want to walk up any more stairs, so she waited till they'd reached the top floor before knocking the kind policeman's cap off, sinking her fingers into his hair, and pulling as hard as she could. The kind policeman dropped her with a thud.

"Ungrateful little madam!" he exclaimed, trying to put his hair and his cap back together. And then, "OH no you don't!" as she came at him with fists flying. He held her off by the wrists.

Angela's mother swiftly put Angela down, and reached a hand into each of Diabola's pockets. She took out the crayons that Diabola had pinched from the hostel and held them out over the wall of the high open-air corridor they were standing in.

Diabola jerked her hands out of the policeman's and thrust them out to her mother, who put two crayons into them silently, a purple one and a red one – Diabola's favourites. She put the others into her own pocket.

Angela looked on admiringly. Her mother was getting cleverer.

Mrs Bashforth had by now unlocked one of the doors leading off the open balcony. It was painted bright blue and had a bubble-glass panel in the top. The glass was cracked and the paint at the bottom of the door was worn to the wood, as if someone had been used to kicking it open.

It opened now with difficulty, scraping along the floor. They all trooped in, including the kind policeman, who wasn't looking at all kind now. The door opened directly into the main room, which seemed also to be the kitchen. Angela and Mrs Cuthbertson-Jones stood in the middle of it, looking round bleakly.

It was a terrible place. There was no furniture apart from a rickety table and two chairs, one broken and on its side, and a sort of armchair with most of the cover gone and the spongy stuff showing.

There was a fireplace but the fire fitting had

been removed.

The wallpaper was hanging off in strips. The floor was too nasty to look at.

The sink was stainless steel which evidently wasn't stainless at all, and badly dented, as if someone had stood in it. There was one tap, and a hole in the sink where the other had been pulled out.

The window, which looked out onto the open walkway, had two panes broken. Angela noticed there was some strange whitish-greenish stuff growing in patches on the walls, and a stain on the ceiling.

"Is this—" Mrs Cuthbertson-Jones cleared her throat to try again, but the council woman chipped in.

"The best we have to offer? You're very lucky to get this."

"I was going to say is this on the top floor?"

"Yes. You're fortunate not to have anyone over your head. There are a lot of musicians in this block," she said ominously. Following Mrs Cuthbertson-Jones' eyes to the damp stains, she added: "These flats are *absolutely weatherproof*. The previous tenants must have had an accident with a pressure-cooker."

Mrs Cuthbertson-Jones gazed round again helplessly, and her eyes met the vicar's.

"Bedrooms?" he asked, trying not to show he was clenching his teeth.

"One. A nice large one."

A door opened straight into it. It was not nice or large, it was long, narrow, and horrid.

"No window?" asked the vicar incredulously, feeling his temper rising in a most un-vicarly manner.

"This was a studio flat," said the woman, as if that explained everything. When they looked blank, she said, "One room." She held up her finger as if they might not know what "one" meant. "The last people wanted a separate bedroom, so they put a partition up. You can take it down if you like." She knocked briskly on the dividing wall, which swayed. "Easily."

"Puff of wind ought to do it," murmured the policeman.

The woman gave him an icy look. "Thank you, Officer," she said coldly. "You must have other things to do."

"Thought the lady might need a ride," he said. The condition of the flat had made him kind again.

"Where to? She lives here now."

Angela, who had been absolutely silent since they left the hostel, suddenly burst into tears.

Everyone in the room (except Diabola, of course) reacted to this in the way people always reacted to Angela crying.

Mrs Cuthbertson-Jones, for whom the sound was literally unbearable and who was at the end of her tether, fled from the room.

The policeman and the vicar rushed to Angela's side, fell on their knees, and began desperately wiping one eye each with big white handkerchiefs so that her small face entirely disappeared.

Mrs Bashforth, who had been as if cut from stone until now, visibly melted into a human being, full of anxiety and distress. She fell on her knees, too, and in trying to hug Angela found herself hugging the policeman and the vicar at the same time. The rest of Angela was lost to view.

Diabola couldn't stand this.

She considered hurling herself onto the group, pummelling and kicking, but three of them were too much. So she jumped on the bed (there was a bed, of sorts, a double divan) and used it like a trampoline. She bounced straight up to the ceiling where she banged her head loudly and fell back unconscious.

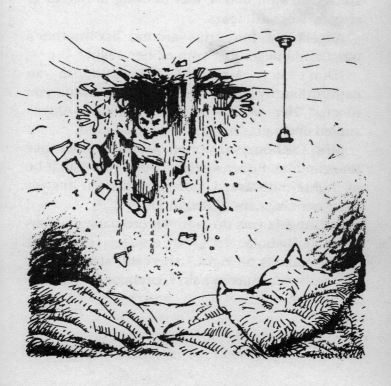

Of course, this was more serious than even Angela's tears. The three comforters had to leave Angela and pay attention to Diabola who was lying on the bed in a rain of plaster, with a large egg rising on top of her head.

The nasty little room was full of exclamations and confusion. Angela pulled herself together and went to find her mother.

She was outside the flat on the walkway. It had started to rain and it was blowing in her face, already wet with tears.

Angela put her arms around her mother's waist and hugged her with all her might.

"Don't cry, Mummy," she said, in an extraordinarily grown-up voice. "I don't want you to cry." Her mother stopped instantly. Angela smiled and said, "It's going to be all right."

Mrs Cuthbertson-Jones gasped down her tears and bent over Angela. "How? How can it be all right?" she asked, not expecting an answer from her six-year-old daughter.

But Angela was no more an ordinary six-year-old than Diabola.

"I'll make it all right," she said, stroking her mother's rain-soaked hair. "I promise."

16. The Vicar Tries Again (And Does Better)

When Diabola had been revived, the council woman fully intended just to walk out of the awful flat and leave them there. She had just said a breezy, "Well, goodbye then!" and headed for the front door, when she found the vicar, small as he was, blocking her way out.

He was so angry by now that he could hardly speak, but managed to utter the one word, "Furniture?"

"I'm afraid that really isn't our responsib—" began Mrs Bashforth.

It was not the vicar who interrupted her, it was the policeman. He had already gone out onto the walkway, where Angela still was. She fixed her large, sad eyes on him compellingly, and to his own surprise he moved in alongside the vicar in the doorway and said very quietly, "I really don't think, madam, that you can expect them to manage with this lot," and he waved his arm around the flat.

"No indeed," said the vicar grimly.

Mrs Bashforth looked around as if for the first time.

"Well!" she said brightly. "It is a little Spartan. Perhaps we might manage a few *pots and pans* from the Council depot... another *chair*." She looked at them hopefully. Neither of them had changed his expression, so she went on rather faintly, "Something for the *floor*, possibly... No promises, mind!" And once more she made an attempt to leave.

The policeman glanced over his shoulder at Angela. He said slowly, "Well, now, I'm off duty... I might just come back with you and see what I could do to – er – hurry things along a little."

Several hours went by. They were a mixture of bad and not so bad for Mrs Cuthbertson-Jones.

The bad part was that Diabola definitely didn't think much of their new home. While her mother was trying to clean up a little – there was a broom of sorts, and some black plastic sacks Mrs Bashforth had left – Diabola expressed her displeasure by smashing another couple of window panes with the heel of her shoe, and trying to set fire to the coverless armchair. This action might well have killed them all with poisonous fumes if her mother had not leapt on her, and dragged her off.

Without the cage, it was difficult to know what

to do with her. Mrs Cuthbertson-Jones was driven to extreme measures. She had already noticed that the stairs carried on upwards, so she bundled Diabola into her mac and dragged her out of the flat, up to the very top of the building, and out onto the flat roof.

Here, as she'd hoped, there was very little damage Diabola could do. There were no glass skylights or anything to smash. Around the roof edge was a low wall. Mrs Cuthbertson-Jones manhandled Diabola to it, lifted her so that she could see over it, and said:

"It's a long way down, Diabola. You don't want to go splat, do you?"

Diabola, peering ten storeys down to the ground, went rigid with fear and shook her head. Her mother set her on her feet.

"All right then. You stay up here and don't go near the edge. Here are your crayons. And there's a nice bit of white wall. I'll come and get you when we've got the flat straight. And don't try to follow me. I'm going to bolt the door to the roof."

"But it's raining! I'll get wet!" wailed Diabola.

"Yes, I'm afraid you will. You should have thought of that before you smashed our windows."

"I've got the matches! I'll burn it all down!"

A quick look round reassured Mrs

Cuthbertson-Jones that there was nothing up here that would burn, unless you counted Diabola, and she was probably too wet. So she shook her off and raced her to the roof-door. She just about got through it in time, and shot the bolt. Diabola hurled herself against it, in vain.

Mrs Cuthbertson-Jones hurried downstairs. As she passed the lift, she stopped. Was that noise the sound of the lift working? It was! After a moment there was a hiss and a clank, and the door opened and the policeman and the vicar stepped out with their arms full of things. The lift was full of things, too. (This is the not-so-bad part of what happened in the next few hours.) From various sources (in the vicar's case, his own home) they had collected the following items: two more kitchen chairs; a rug; an electric heater; some bedding; a frying-pan, two saucepans, three plates, mugs, knives, forks and spoons; a box of food; some warm clothes and some books and pictures. (The policeman thought these were a waste of space but the vicar said they were necessities of life.)

In addition, the policeman had brought some tools and pieces of cardboard to board up the broken windows. (Of course there were more of these now, but luckily he'd brought enough.)

The four of them worked for several hours. Angela too. She wasn't very used to working, but she tried. She spread sheets and a quilt on the double divan bed in the bedroom. While she did it, she was thinking uneasily, "Who's going to sleep here?"

The thought of actually sleeping with Dybo in the same bed was naturally not a pleasant one.

When she'd finished, she was quite puffed, and sat down for a minute. She was not feeling good. She slowly realised that what she felt was a sort of shadow (but a very dark one) of what Dybo was feeling, up on the roof in the rain. Angela might be uneasy and miserable, but at least she was dry and warm. After a while she tried to send some of that dryness and warmth to Dybo.

How did she do this? The way you send your thoughts to someone. You concentrate on them. You wish. You hope. You focus on them in your mind. That was what Angela did.

And up on the roof, a furious, wet, cold, abandoned Diabola felt a sudden warm glow. Her thoughts of revenge and destruction melted. No, not exactly melted. It was as if her brain were a cold deadly ball, like a planet made of steel spikes all pointing outward and suddenly a very hot little meteor landed among the spikes and melted a patch in them.

The meteor was Angela's thoughts. And Diabola instantly knew this. She knew where the glow had come from. She knew that Angela had sent her this present because she was good, so good she didn't want Dybo to be cold and wet.

This made Diabola so *furious* that she tore off her mac and threw it over the wall into the street below. Then she flung herself down in the biggest puddle she could find, rolled about in it until she was soaked to the skin, and then lay there, panting, staring up at the raining sky, sending the coldest, wettest, wickedest thoughts she could, straight back to her sister.

The warm glow faded and the spikes returned. Sharper than ever.

"Mummy!"

"Yes, darling?"

"I'm cold!"

Angela never complained. But now she was shivering from head to foot and her skin felt clammy. Her mother, the vicar and the policeman all gathered round her. The policeman took off his jacket and wrapped her in it. The vicar rubbed her hands between his own warm ones. Mrs Cuthbertson-Jones hugged her.

"Are you ill, Angela?"

Angela shook her head.

"It's D-d-d-dybo," she said between chattering teeth. "She's up there on the r-r-r-roof. Please get her down!"

Mrs Cuthbertson-Jones sent the policeman upstairs. As he opened the roof-door, something like a small, sopping wet torpedo struck him amidships. He just managed to save himself from falling backwards down the stairs.

He carried her down under his arm, ignoring her kicks and struggles. A policeman sees lots of fairly bad people so he was not too put out – he had always thought that badness starts in childhood. He didn't even think it odd that the mother, who had run a warm bath while he'd been gone, thrust the child into it without undressing her. He wouldn't have cared to try taking her clothes off, risking those teeth and those nails.

It wasn't until later that night when he took his own clothes off, that he discovered he was covered with bruises, and his hair where she'd pulled it wouldn't lie right for weeks.

By nightfall, the flat was just about fit to live in. There was a rug on the floor; the pictures were up; the heater was on; the windows boarded; the table laid. Some baked beans and bacon were cooking (there was a stove in the flat, though only one of the burners worked).

Mrs Cuthbertson-Jones invited the vicar to eat with them, but he made his excuses. He was worried about his cat. But he looked into the bedroom before he left. Angela was sitting on the floor reading one of the books.

"Will you be all right?" he asked tenderly.

"I'm going to try to be," she answered rather oddly. She reached up her small hand. "What's your name?"

"Er – Benedict," he said. He took her hand. The glow that Diabola had rejected now flowed into the vicar like a blessing. He felt all choked up - it was so much more than he felt he deserved.

"I'll be back tomorrow to see how your dear mother is getting on," he said.

"Thank you, Benedict," said Angela, so sweetly that he had to turn away to hide his tears.

The arrangement at bedtime – the only possible one

– was that Mrs Cuthbertson-Jones slept in the middle of the divan, with a twin on each side.

Angela kissed her mother and said, "It's nice like this," and fell instantly asleep, cuddled up at her side.

Diabola was also exhausted, luckily. She had time for only two pinches and a kick before she began to snore like a walrus.

Mrs Cuthbertson-Jones thought about what the vicar had said. That Diabola and Angela being together, without the extra good person (their father), might have brought their old house crashing down. And suddenly a terrible thought occurred to her.

The terrible thought was helped along – perhaps it was caused – by a very slight movement of the bed. A sort of tiny shiver. As if the whole block of flats had trembled.

Perhaps it was just an earth tremor. But no! It wasn't! Mrs Cuthbertson-Jones knew, deep inside her, that this tremor was not natural. It was very unnatural indeed.

Her eyes flew to Diabola. She could see her by the light of a nightlight the vicar had brought. Her spiky hair made weird flickering shadows on the dingy walls. Her face was creased in a scowl and between snores she made small yelping noises. They sounded like the noises dogs make when they catch rabbits in their dreams. A sort of excited, triumphant noise.

But she was asleep. Fast asleep. It couldn't be her, doing the tremor!

Or could it?

She had been asleep when their house fell down, too. Maybe – was such a thing possible? Could Diabola, in her dreams, be *willing* something terrible to happen?

Mrs Cuthbertson-Jones found herself sitting sharply upright in bed. Her skin had turned to goosebumps and her scalp was prickling.

What if this whole block fell down?

Whether Diabola was doing it, or whether she was just causing it because there weren't enough good people to balance her, hardly mattered. If this whole ten-storey block came crashing down, they would all be killed for sure. And what about all the other people in it?

The tiny tremor was a warning. Mrs Cuthbertson-Jones must do something! But what? What? She felt absolutely desperate suddenly. Desperately frightened and desperately alone.

Suddenly she had a worse thought – worse even than the block crashing down. It was this. If Diabola could make so much mischief when she was just a child, what about when she'd grown up? Mrs Cuthbertson-Jones was filled with panic.

Oh, where was her husband? Why wasn't he here? Not that she blamed him for running away. She wanted to run away herself.

Unexpectedly she heard Angela's voice at her side.

"Mummy," she said, "we have to find Daddy."

More goosebumps! Had Angela heard her mother's thoughts, in her sleep?

"How?"

"Aren't there people who look for people?"

Mrs Cuthbertson-Jones thought wildly. "The Salvation Army! They sometimes find missing people."

"Let's ask them to find him and bring him back."

"He might not want to come back."

"But if he did, he couldn't find us, now. Now we're not at home. We must let him know where we are. We need him!"

"We certainly need somebody. Somebody – very,

very good."

"Daddy's good!"

"Somebody whose goodness is stronger than Daddy's."

And into her head it came – unbidden, but irresistible. The best person she knew.

The vicar! The vicar! If she could get him to come and live with them, they might be able to balance Diabola.

But how could it happen, that the vicar would come to live with them?

The answer came to her with shocking clearness.

"Angela!"

"What, Mummy?"

"Do you think the vicar – likes me?"

"Yes. He calls you a dear lady."

"That doesn't mean anything."

"Benedict really likes you. I know he does."

Benedict? A beautiful name. With a beautiful meaning – blessed. Yes! Perhaps it was fate!

"Go to sleep now, darling. I have to think."

"Salvation Army…" murmured Angela. She snuggled down. "Mummy," she said, her little voice suddenly anxious, "you will wake up early in the morning? Before Dybo?"

"Don't worry, I will."

And Angela fell asleep again. She always did as she was told.

But her mother hardly slept all night.

17. Diabola Develops New Skills

The next morning, their new life really began.

Mrs Cuthbertson-Jones got up early. It was still dark in the room. The nightlight had burnt out, and as there was no window, the only light came from the next room – and even that wasn't much, with the boarded-up windows.

However, that was good in a way, because Diabola usually woke up at dawn, and this time she stayed asleep. Her mother was afraid to leave her alone with Angela. She lifted her carefully out of bed, carried her into the main room, and tied her to one of the chairs with strips of black plastic sack. She didn't tie her tight. It was just instead of the cage, while she got the breakfast.

The room was dark because of the boarded-up windows. She tried to turn on the only light – a bulb hanging from the ceiling. It had worked all right last night, but now it gave a little pop and went out. So she opened the door onto the open walkway to let in some light, and began frying sausages.

Pretty soon she had her first visit from her new neighbours.

Two young men put their heads round the open door. They were not very nice or clean-looking young men, in fact they looked as if they had been out in the rain all night. One of them had a shaven head.

"'Ullo, dorling," said that one, leering at her. "Need any 'elp wiv the cookin'?"

"No, thank you," said Mrs Cuthbertson-Jones.

"Goin' to invite us in to breakfast?"

"No," said Mrs Cuthbertson-Jones.

They both came in anyway.

"Nice place you got 'ere," said the shaven-headed one, jumping up and pulling off one of the polystyrene ceiling-tiles.

"I don't think it's nice," said Mrs Cuthbertson-Jones. "Please stop that."

"Y'-wot?"

"Aaaaow! Ay don't think it's naice!" said the other. "D'you 'ear that? She don't think it's naice!"

"Our block ain't good enough for her, that it?" said the shaven-headed one, coming much too close to her. She could smell drink on his breath and she began to feel very alarmed.

She didn't notice Diabola opening her eyes.

The young visitors didn't notice her at all, in the dim light.

160

The other young man, the one with hair, put his foot against the edge of the table. The table moved along the floor. He seemed to think this was fun, and gave it a good kick.

Mrs Cuthbertson-Jones felt even more frightened. She suddenly missed Mr Cuthbertson-Jones very much indeed.

"Would you please get out of my flat?" she asked. But she asked it in a weak, trembly voice, not her new, stronger one.

"Ow, she don't want us!"

"Well, she shouldn'ta left the door open!"

"Yeah! Invitin' us in, that was, good as!"

"Oooh, look! Bangers! Let's be 'avin' one!" And the young man who'd been drinking (well, they both had, actually) plucked one of the sausages from the frying-pan.

Diabola had been watching all this from her corner. She wasn't properly awake yet. She couldn't understand who these men were. She saw nothing wrong with their behaviour, but they were in her space. She moved her arms and legs uneasily against the plastic strips. She felt she was going to need them in a minute. Her arms and legs, that is.

The young man with the sausage let out a yell.

"Cor! It's 'ot!"

He threw it across the room.

It hit Diabola on the nose.

That decided her. She was against these intruders. But she was also tied up and helpless.

The two young men were gaping at her. They had only just spotted her. They could see she was tied up. They couldn't understand it.

They didn't have long to try.

Diabola did what she'd done yesterday, up on the roof, when Angela's warm-up thoughts had hit her. She didn't know exactly how she had done what she did. She just did it again. She focused her anger on the two young men on the other side of the room.

The one with hair felt it stand up on end.

The one without, felt goosepimples pop out all over him.

Then they both felt something else.

They felt as if they were having two neat holes drilled through their chests.

They let out simultaneous howls.

One of them shouted, "I'm shot!"

The other one bawled, "She got me!"

They clutched their chests, turned tail and fled, yelling blue murder.

Diabola, by mistake, had done her first good thing.

Her mother slammed the door shut, then rushed to her and released her. She was almost in tears. In her confusion she thought Diabola had done whatever she'd done, for *her*. So she hugged her and cried, "Thank you, darling, thank you!"

Diabola, utterly unused to being hugged, jumped back, glaring at her mother. For a moment, her mother felt the power of those eyes, as the young men had. But then Diabola realised. No. This was her carer. Without a carer, someone to cook for her and look after her, she would be more uncomfortable and unsafe than she was. She dropped her eyes and the bad feeling Mrs Cuthbertson-Jones had begun to have, went away.

But Diabola had seen (as she hadn't seen yesterday) what her angry thoughts had been able to do. She stored this away in her brain.

The girls ate breakfast together in silence.

After eating her sausages, Angela said timidly, "Are we going to school, Mummy?"

"I don't know," said her mother. "It's a long way from here."

"I must go to school," said Diabola. "You must take me to school."

"How?" asked her mother. She didn't expect an answer, but Diabola instantly said, "In a taxi."

"I haven't enough money for taxis."

"You'll have to get some," said Diabola.

"How?" asked her mother again in the same helpless way.

"Steal it, of course," said Diabola.

Angela gave a little cry.

"I can't do that," said her mother. She didn't say it reproachfully. It was useless to reproach Diabola, and anyway, she wasn't surprised at the suggestion. She was just stating a fact.

Diabola glared at her and then got up from the table and went to the bathroom.

She put the lid of the toilet down and climbed onto it. There was a small window just there. It opened onto the public walkway outside the flat. It was too small for anyone over the age of seven to climb through. But Diabola wasn't over the age of seven, so she climbed through it, and dropped down onto the walkway.

She ran along the walkway to the lift. She'd noticed the day before how pressing the button made the lift come. So she did that. The lift came, the doors opened obligingly, Diabola went in, the doors shut. She waited for the lift to take her to the ground.

It didn't.

She waited. She began to get worried. She didn't know how to make the lift move or how to make the doors open. But luckily (for her) someone down on the ground floor pressed the button, and the lift began to move.

When the lift reached the ground floor, the doors opened and Diabola found herself facing a large, kindly-looking woman with some shopping.

"Hullo, dear," said this woman. "You're not supposed to play in the lift, you know." She didn't sound cross, but Diabola didn't like being told what she was not supposed to do.

She thought of trying out her new eye-thing that she'd done to the young men, but then she decided not to. The woman lived in the same block of flats as she did. She might cause trouble. So Diabola just said, "You're not supposed to not mind your own business."

Before the large kindly woman could work this out, Diabola had gone past her and outdoors.

She found herself in a street where quite a lot of people were coming and going. Diabola stood aside and watched them. After a short time she noticed a man who looked rather better-dressed than most of the others. Diabola walked up to him.

"Give me some money," she said.

The man stopped and stared at her.

"You cheeky little monkey," he said. "Just like that! If you want to beg, you'll have to learn to do it better!"

And he started to walk past her.

"Stop," she said.

Oddly enough, he did. He didn't look round at her. He just stopped. Diabola said, "Give me some money and I won't hurt you."

The man was absolutely astounded. He was a big, strong man, who thought a lot of himself. Yet here was this small girl threatening him. He didn't know how to take it. So he tried to walk on.

He didn't get far, of course.

He felt a most peculiar sensation in his back. A boring sensation. Not of being bored. Of being bored *into*.

He stopped dead with a shout, and put his hand up to feel his back.  There was nothing there. But he still felt bored-into, as if someone were pushing a pole through him. He spun round.

The little girl was still there. She had her eyes fixed on his middle. The boring-into feeling had transferred itself to his tummy. It was such a strong feeling, he looked down to see if his tummy-button had become a tunnel leading straight through to the back.

167

"Give me some money," said the dead little voice again.

The man reached swiftly into his breast pocket and brought out his wallet. He was sweating. His teeth were chattering.

"H – how much do you want?" he asked.

He shouldn't have said that.

"All of it."

He was quite convinced by now that he had a hole right through him. It was a terrifying feeling. With trembling hands he drew out all the notes he had in his wallet. She walked up to him and took them.

The bored-into feeling stopped as if switched off. It was so sudden and complete, he wondered if he'd dreamt it.

"Just a moment, you—!" he shouted. But Diabola had turned and was running like mad. The man looked at his empty wallet, swallowed several times, bent over to look at his stomach, and then made his way hurriedly to the nearest pub for a stiff drink.

Except of course that he had no money to pay for it.

When Diabola got back to the flat, she found she couldn't climb back into the little window, so she knocked on the door.

She'd only been gone a few minutes. Her

mother hadn't even missed her. So she was quite surprised on opening the front door to find Diabola standing there.

"Diabola! Where have you been?"

"Getting some money for the taxi," she said. She handed her mother a ten–pound note. She didn't show her the rest of the money, which she had hidden.

Mrs Cuthbertson-Jones stared at the note in horror.

"Where did you get it?" she asked in a whisper. "You didn't steal it, did you?"

"No," said Diabola. "A man gave it to me."

"He *gave* it to you? Why should he?"

"I told him to."

She pushed past and went to collect her things for school.

It's hard to describe Mrs Cuthbertson-Jones' feelings about this incident. Never, perhaps, has the sight of a much-needed ten-pound note frightened a mother so much. It seemed to her that a big leap had been taken. Into more and worse badness.

Whether Diabola had stolen the money, or begged it, or demanded it with menaces, she must have got it by some bad means. But "bad" was not the first word in Mrs Cuthbertson-Jones's thoughts. She was remembering the two young men who had fled, screaming, and the word that came first was... unnatural.

Going out for a few minutes and coming back with a crisp new ten-pound note could not just happen naturally. Not in this day and age.

When the girls appeared, ready for school, she said, "I'll take you on the bus."

"Taxi," said Diabola. Her eyes had gone glittery.

"I can't use this money, Diabola," said her mother firmly. "It isn't ours."

The little green eyes narrowed dangerously. But then she shrugged and walked out by herself. Her mother rushed after her.

"Where are you going?"

"To school," said Diabola without turning round, walking along the corridor. "In a taxi."

"Taxi drivers won't pick up little girls!"

Diabola stopped. After a moment she turned round. She was about six metres from her mother. She said in a low, compelling voice, "Then you must come."

Her mother opened her mouth to refuse. But quite suddenly she had a blinding headache, so bad she reeled and fell against the wall.

Angela was beside her.

"Mummy! What's wrong?"

"My head – my head...!"

Angela reached up both hands and laid them

on her head. The pain eased. But the fear didn't.

"Mummy, do what she says," whispered Angela.

Without another word, they went down to street level. Mrs Cuthbertson-Jones hailed a passing taxi and took them to school in it.

When they arrived, they got out, and the taxi man said, "Three pounds eighty."

It was only then that Mrs Cuthbertson-Jones realised she not only hadn't brought the ten pounds. She hadn't brought any money at all.

"Oh dear – I forgot to bring any— " she began, all of a fluster.

Diabola looked at the taxi man, but decided it wasn't worth tiring herself with her eye-thing. It needed too much concentration. So she reached under her skirt. Out of her knickers she brought a large roll of money. She peeled off a note and gave it to him, and without waiting for change or anything else, walked off up the path to the school.

The taxi man wasted no time. He muttered, "Blimey! I'll be winnin' the lottery next!" pocketed the note and drove away.

Angela and her mother were left staring after Diabola.

"What shall I do?" whispered Mrs Cuthbertson-Jones.

"Ask Benedict," Angela said. But she was staring in an oddly fixed way after the retreating taxi. "Goodbye, Mummy. See you after school." And she hurried after Diabola.

Mrs Cuthbertson-Jones stood on the kerbside, utterly bewildered and helpless, miles from home and without her purse.

Suddenly the same taxi, which had dwindled to a dot down the street, could be seen undwindling, in fact getting larger and closer. It must have done a U-turn.

It drew up beside her.

"Excuse me, madam," said the taxi man slowly. He looked rather dazed, as if he'd just woken up. "Your – your little girl gave me far too much. Enough to pay for your journey home, if – if – "

They stared at each other. He was seeing her, not as the sort of customer who can't afford tips, but as a forlorn lady who needed his help. She was seeing him, not as a hard-hearted taxi driver, but as a kind man offering just what she needed.

She smiled at him. He smiled back and got out to open the door for her. Wordlessly, she climbed in and asked him to take her back to the block of flats.

On the way, Mrs Cuthbertson-Jones heard him singing a rather strange song:

"I feel so happy!
I feel so nice!
I wish I could buy this dear lady
An ice!
All the world's troubles
Have drifted a-way!
Everything's friendly,
So happy and—"

He broke off, and she heard him mutter, "Dear oh dear, I can't think of a rhyme!"

Something in the song reminded his passenger of what she had been thinking of, half the night. She leant forward and tapped the glass partition.

"Could you take me to the vicarage instead?"

So he did. When they arrived, he gave her the exact change from the two trips and refused to take a tip.

The vicar was both pleased and alarmed to see her. He asked her in and gave her a cup of hot tea.

She had never been in a vicarage before. This one was small, cosy and plain, with very few little touches of homeliness – rather sad, really, she thought; no curtains, only blinds; no flowers, or family photographs; very few ornaments or trinkets or souvenirs of holidays. But there was a nice warm fire and there was the cat, which jumped on her lap and began to purr.

Stroking it soothed her. She would have liked another cat. She found herself wishing she could swop Diabola for a nice little cat. So simple. You knew just where you were, with cats. This horribly unmotherly thought made her want to cry, but she was getting braver and stronger all the time, so she didn't.

Instead she told the vicar about the money, and about what had happened in the night.

"The bed trembled," she said. "Vicar, what's to stop the whole block collapsing? If what you said is right?"

"Oh good heavens! I never thought of that!" exclaimed the vicar in horror. "All those people! It doesn't bear thinking of!"

"Someone good must come and live with us," she said. "For balance, as you explained."

"That's right!" he agreed eagerly. "That would be your husband, of course. We must find him. The Salvation Army, you know, is very good at finding lost—"

"Well," said Mrs Cuthbertson-Jones slowly. "I

was thinking more of... someone... with more goodness than my husband."

"Who could that be?"

She mustered all her courage. "You," she said.

Blushing hotly, she raised her eyes to his face.

He looked... Well, he looked like a man who has just received his first proposal of marriage, when it was the very last thing he expected. Extremely surprised. But also, extremely happy.

He couldn't think of a thing to say. But his hands knew what to do. They reached out without his order, took the one of hers that was stroking the cat, and just held it. The three hands clasped on its back were too heavy for the cat, who leapt to the floor.

"My dear lady," he said at last. "Do you mean – what I think you mean?"

Mrs Cuthbertson-Jones was still only about twenty-eight years old. She had had a hard time, but this had not affected her looks. She was very pretty and had soft, gentle ways. Now the vicar thought about it, he realised he had admired her long ago when she used to sit in church every Sunday at her husband's side. He realised that the reason he had been so anxious to help the family yesterday was not just a vicarly reason. It was a manly reason too.

He let go of her hand and covered his eyes.

"Oh dear, oh dear," he murmured. "I am not as good as you think me. Surely what we should try to do is to find your husband and persuade him to return to you?"

Which, of course, only goes to show what a very good, unselfish, decent sort he actually was.

18. Diabola Develops More Skills

Meanwhile, at school, Angela was learning as hard as she could in the classroom while Diabola was missing regular lessons to have her special art lesson with Mrs Kirkbright.

The headmistress, after settling "dear Dybo" down with her art materials, had suggested that she give battle scenes a rest and draw something everyday, like, well, like a building. She then slipped out of the room for a few minutes. Diabola immediately began drawing a picture of the block of flats they now lived in.

She made it exactly ten storeys high, like the real one. She put in the windows and open corridors and the steps and then, in the middle, she put in the lift (though, really, you couldn't see that from the outside). She finished it by putting a straight line on top for the roof.

Then she took her paints. She was allowed to use poster colours now because she was getting on so well, and she had a box of little jars of different colours. She dipped her brush carefully into one of the jars. It was orange, a lovely bright flame colour, just exactly what she wanted, because she now proceeded to paint in a lot of flames.

They were coming out of the open corridors and out of the windows, long tongues of fire. She took another brush and added some red to make it look hotter. It looked really as if the building were burning.

She blew on the paint to dry it. Then she took a black pen and began to draw people in the building.

This was the best part, because they were all standing out on the balconies and leaning from the windows, waving their arms and screaming their heads off because they were burning to death. She even put in the kindly lady from this morning. She was trapped in the lift with her shopping.

Diabola drew two last figures. They were on the roof. The fire hadn't got there yet. It was just licking round the edges. It would soon reach those two people, the big one and the small one...

Mrs Kirkbright had returned to her room, quietly to avoid disturbing her little genius. Now she was leaning over Diabola's shoulder.

"Dybo, dear, that's wonderful! How realistic! How horrific! Why, it makes me feel quite terrified to—"

But her praises stopped short. There was a

silence while Diabola went on drawing. Then a finger came down and pointed.

"Those two people on the roof, dear – they look rather like…"

Now Diabola was putting in their hair. Dark hair on the big figure. Fair, curly hair on the little figure, who seemed to be wearing school uniform. They both wore expressions of alarm.

"Dybo," said Mrs Kirkbright slowly. "That's – that's not your mummy and your sister is it?"

"Yes," said Diabola.

She picked up the orange brush again in one hand, and the red brush in the other, and using them together, she began to paint very quickly. Her breath was coming in short gasps and her eyes were glistening with excitement. The flames were creeping up over the roof. They were surrounding the two figures. They were…

"Dybo! Stop!" Genius or no genius, this was too much! "No, dear, you mustn't! It's too cruel! I shall take your paints away!"

Diabola stopped dead.

For a second she thought of eye-thing-ing Mrs Kirkbright. She wanted to very badly. But Mrs Kirkbright was useful to her. If she hurt or frightened her too much, Diabola might not be allowed to do her pictures. She might be made to learn boring things all day instead.

She stared down at the picture, holding back

her desire to do the eye-thing to Mrs Kirkbright. She felt inside her a powerful frustration. And this strong, held-back feeling caused something very extraordinary to happen.

The middle of the picture began to go black.

At first it was just a little black spot. But smoke began to rise from it, and then, quite quickly, the black spot spread until the middle of the building in the drawing was blacked-out and the smoke was getting into Diabola's eyes.

Mrs Kirkbright gasped. The paper – the paper was smouldering!

Before she could grasp what was happening, the edges of the black spot burst into flames. Real flames!

The headmistress screamed, grabbed a register off her desk, and slammed it down on top of the painting.

This put the fire out. *Apparently*.

The headmistress stared at Diabola, who was still looking down at the table.

"Dybo," she whispered. "Did – did you do that?"

"Spon… spontaneous combustion," said Diabola.

"I – I beg your pardon?"

"It was spon… spontaneous combustion," repeated Diabola.

Mrs Kirkbright was speechless. After a moment she recovered her voice. "How do you know about spontaneous combustion?" she asked.

"It means when something catches fire by itself," said Diabola.

"I know what it means. How do you know what it means?"

Mrs Kirkbright had never spoken to her in that tone before. A fearful, suspicious tone. Diabola quickly looked up to see what Mrs Kirkbright was looking like. She made her eyes a harmless blank. She found she could do this.

"I read it in a book," she said.

This was, of course, a lie. She had no idea where the words had come from. She had needed them and there they were, on her tongue.

Mrs Kirkbright found that she had backed away several paces. This would not do! She came forward again, and picked up the big book she had used to put the burning page out with.

But as she picked it up she dropped it with a cry, because it was extremely hot.

So hot, in fact, that as it landed on the floor of her office, it burst into flames. The flames quickly spread to the carpet.

The headmistress seized Diabola by the wrist and tried to drag her from the room, but Diabola was staring at the burning book. She seemed rooted to the floor. As Mrs Kirkbright pulled at her arm, she pulled back and Mrs Kirkbright nearly fell over.

"Dybo!" she screamed. "Come – come quickly – I must call the fire brigade – come away from the fire!"

Diabola looked at her. Her eyes were no longer harmless and blank. The flames from the burning floor were reflected in them.

The sight suddenly filled Mrs Kirkbright with unreasoning mortal terror. Before she could remind herself that she was leaving a little helpless child in a burning room, she had turned and fled.

Diabola watched the spreading flames for another few moments. Then, quite calmly, she gathered up her art materials and put them into her schoolbag. She glanced at the picture of the block of flats. It had a hole the size of her fist burnt into the middle of it. But the two little figures on the roof were still there.

With the real flames spreading and the smoke half-choking her, she quickly stuck her forefingers into the pots of red and orange paint – there was no time to use brushes. She finger-painted big, fat flames around the figures. She smeared the red and orange all over them until they disappeared.

Then she lifted the picture and threw it onto the blazing floor.

Real flames… paint flames…

You could no longer tell which was which.

19. Angela Takes a Hand

The school did not burn to the ground, not quite. Fortunately, Mrs Kirkbright was able to give the alarm in time.

There was a lot of confusion, of course. The fire alarm went off; classes were hurried out into the playground. The teachers made hasty attempts to rescue their possessions. Several children who'd been smoking in the lavatories got more smoke than they'd bargained for. The caretaker, a bad-tempered man who was hated by everyone, later won an award for bravery for dashing back into the smoke-filled building. He ignored the coughing from the lavatories and rescued several valuable computers.

Meanwhile Diabola slipped out through a window, caught a taxi, and guided the driver back to the block of flats. It turned out not to be true that taxi drivers won't pick up small children – at least, not when the small children hail them by waving twenty-pound notes.

On the way home, she did some thinking. It had been a very exciting day. She realised now that she had Powers. She wasn't sure yet what they were, exactly, but she knew she had them. The main thing was to find out more about them.

All the way home in the taxi she was wondering if just by drawing something, she could make it happen. The event at the school had made her hungry for a really good, really *real* fire. The thought of the block of flats in flames was thrilling. Perhaps it was already a burnt-out shell?

But when the taxi rounded the last bend, she saw that the block was just as she had left it. So she paid the taxi man (not being nice like the other one, he tried to get away without giving her change, but she just gave him a brief zap of eye-power and he paid up, gasping and holding his nose) and hurried inside and up in the lift.

She knocked on the door. Her mother opened it a crack, and then all the way.

"Diabola! What are you doing here?"

"The school's on fire," Diabola answered, pushing past her.

"THE SCHOOL'S ON FIRE! Oh no! What about Angela?"

"I expect she's burnt up. Where's lunch?"

Poor Mrs Cuthbertson-Jones was frantic. She had no phone. She rushed to the next-door flat and knocked.

Luckily for her, it was the kindly woman with the shopping that Diabola had met that morning outside the lift.

"Hullo, dear," she said. "You just moved in next door, am I right? I should have—"

"Please – please –" gasped Mrs Cuthbertson-Jones. "Have you a phone?"

"Yes, dear, would you like to—?"

But her distraught neighbour had already burst past her and seized the phone in the passage. She rang the school number which she knew by heart. Oddly enough, it rang, and even more oddly, it was answered. The bad-tempered caretaker happened to be in the main office, loading up with electronic equipment.

"Yers, wotcha want?"

"Is that the school?"

"What's left of it."

"Oh, my God! Where are the children?"

"The children? Who cares? Save the computers, that's what I say. They're our future, after all." And he hung up.

Mrs Cuthbertson-Jones turned to her new neighbour and blurted out what had happened. "I have to go there!" she cried. "My daughter—"

"Course you do, dear, that's all right. I'll mind the other one for you, shall I? Off you go, we'll be fine, what's her name then?"

But Mrs Cuthbertson-Jones was already dashing for the lift. She wasn't thinking clearly. When she got into the street, she was astonished to see a taxi standing at the kerb right outside the block, as if waiting for her.

As she approached, she was even more amazed to find that the driver was the same one as this morning.

Having left her at the vicarage, he was just as surprised to see her.

"What are you doing here?" she asked him.

"Don't ask me," he replied, still in that rather dazed voice. "I was just pickin' up a fare by the precinct when I – I –" He passed a hand across his brow. "I had, like, a call. Somethin' just – made me come here."

"Please – take me back to the school!"

He raced her there. "Strike a light!" he exclaimed as they rounded the corner.

The street was full of fire-engines; great hoses were snaking everywhere, pumping and jumping. Out in the playground scores of children and a dozen teachers were milling about. There was a lot of noise and a lot of water and a lot of smoke.

Mrs Cuthbertson-Jones leapt out of the taxi and ran into the school yard. She picked out Ms Applebough and rushed through the crowd to her side.

"Ms Applebough! Where's Angela?"

Ms Applebough gazed round at the pool of children surrounding her.

"Why, she was here a moment ago—"

"You mean – she's gone?"

"Don't worry, Mrs Cuthbertson-Jones! She's safe and sound! She must have drifted away to watch the fire fighters."

But she hadn't, because her mother combed the whole playground and asked everyone, including, at last, Mrs Kirkbright, who was standing staring at the burning wing that had contained her office.

"Mrs Kirkbright! Have you seen Angela?"

"No," the headmistress replied, turning slowly to face Mrs Cuthbertson-Jones. "But I've seen Dybo. Oh yes. I've seen her all right!"

Even through her anxiety, Mrs Cuthbertson-Jones gave a start. The headmistress had never used that grim tone when speaking about Diabola.

"What... what's happened?" the poor mother asked fearfully.

"Who do you think, Mrs Cuthbertson-Jones," asked Mrs Kirkbright slowly and deliberately, "set my school on fire?"

"Oh – no. Oh no."

"Oh but oh yes. And I hold you entirely responsible. You should have warned me."

At this moment Mrs Cuthbertson-Jones felt a tap on her shoulder. It was the taxi man.

"Your little girl's waitin' for you, love," he said in a soft, dreamy voice.

"What?"

"Little darlin's sittin' in my cab. Waitin' for 'er mum."

Angela was sitting primly in the back of the taxi. She hadn't a hair out of place, and her schoolbag was beside her. When her mother fell on her and hugged her breathless, she just sat there until she'd finished and then said, "We must go now, Mummy."

"Go? Where?" asked her mother in bewilderment. "Home?"

"No. We have to find Daddy. We have to."

Mrs Cuthbertson-Jones sat beside her with one arm around her. It was so comforting, such a tremendous relief, to have her sweet angel-child safe and with her that she hardly heard what she was saying or noticed where they were going.

But the taxi man had had his orders. He drove them for several miles through the city streets and pulled up at a building that might once have been a small church. Over the door it said "Salvation Army".

"I meant to come alone, after school," Angela explained. "I think I could have managed by myself, now." Her mother stared at her, frowning. She seemed to be getting less and less childlike.

"But you couldn't—"

"But you would have worried... Anyway when I saw you in the playground I knew you'd come to help me. Like the nice taxi man."

The taxi man couldn't hear them through the glass partition, but nevertheless he suddenly burst into a rousing hymn:

"An-gel come to earth from 'eaven
Pure of 'eart and free from sin –
Fills my soul wiv joy and gladness
Which, be-fower, was in the bin!"

Angela smiled tenderly.

Then she got out of the taxi, told him he had a beautiful singing voice ("Wotcha mean, miss, I can't sing a note!") and asked him to wait. She led her mother through the doors of the building, and soon Mrs Cuthbertson-Jones found herself filling out a form describing her husband, telling when he had gone missing, and so on.

"Well, I think this shouldn't be too hard," said the Sally Army man. "Now go home and wait patiently and we'll be in touch."

Angela fixed her eyes on him.

"Will you please be as quick as you can, finding him?"

The man opened his mouth and then closed it again. He couldn't look away from Angela. She added solemnly, "Bridges."

"I beg your pardon?"

"Try underneath bridges," she said.

They climbed back in the taxi which at once drove off in the direction of home. As they sat there in silence, Mrs Cuthbertson-Jones was thinking, "And if they do find him, and if he does come back... What shall I do about Benedict?"

The taxi man was still singing at the top of his voice:

"Oh so good, and oh so lovely!
Straight from paradise she come!
And I got 'er in my taxi,
Sitting back there wiv 'er Mum!"

20. On the Roof

Mrs Cuthbertson-Jones had been too stressed to give a thought to the fate of the kindly neighbour who'd offered to look after Diabola, but when they got back to the flat they found a scene of devastation.

The door was hanging open as if someone had beat a headlong retreat. Inside the kitchen-living-room, chairs lay on their sides, the table was askew, there were splashes on the walls and broken glass on the floor. The last two window panes had been shattered.

One look in the bedroom and bathroom disclosed that Diabola was not there. But the bathroom wall had a drawing on it. It showed a figure who was unmistakably the kindly neighbour, with her eyes crossed, her tongue sticking out, and a large nail right through her head.

With an exclamation of horror, Mrs Cuthbertson-Jones rushed next door. She knocked. From inside she heard gibbering noises, and, when she knocked again, a voice screamed:

"NO! NO! Go away! Leave me alone! I'm calling the police – the fire brigade – the council vermin-exterminator! Get away from me, you horrible, horrible little fiend!"

Then she heard the sound of a large piece of furniture being dragged across the floor and rammed against the inside of the door. The light in the door-window was blocked out.

Mrs Cuthbertson-Jones went back to her own flat, where she found Angela quietly sweeping up the glass.

"Where do you think she is?" asked Mrs Cuthbertson-Jones.

"Perhaps she's out practising."

"Practising? Practising what?" asked her mother fearfully.

Angela straightened up and looked her mother in the eye.

"Things have changed," she said.

"Yes," said Mrs Cuthbertson-Jones under her breath.

"I've changed since the house fell down. Dybo's changed too. We haven't got different. Only – more so."

"You feel it?"

"Yes, I feel it. I'm getting stronger. I have to, so I am. But she is, too."

"But – practising?"

"I have to practise, too. There's lots I could do.

You saw the taxi driver. That was me. I changed him. Dybo can do things like that. Only the opposite."

"The money?"

"Yes."

"The fire?"

"Yes."

"Maybe the house?"

"Oh, yes."

"Is she – very strong? She's not... not stronger than you, is she?"

"I don't know."

"So what shall we do?"

"We must find her."

"How?"

"She can't go far away from me. We're meant to be close to each other."

She stood for a long moment with her eyes shut. Her mother looked at her. In the middle of the dreary, devastated room, so dark and gloomy, Angela seemed to shine with her own light. She put out love and peace and beauty and calm, like visible rays. These rays reached her mother, and the dread and guilt, the hopelessness and desperation, dropped away, leaving her calm and peaceful too. (And beautiful. But of course she didn't know that. Mr Cuthbertson-Jones, if he'd been there, would have noticed it. So would Benedict.)

After a time, Angela opened her eyes.

"She's up there," she said, pointing at the ceiling.

"Up where?"

"On the roof."

From the rooftop, Diabola could just see the column of smoke from the distant school, still trickling upward and lying in a flat, dirty cloud above their old district.

She looked at it with satisfaction for some time. It was the best feeling she'd ever felt (well, the worst, which was the best for her).

After a while she thought of trying an experiment. She fixed her eyes on a small shop on the corner of the street, just below the block.

It was a long way down – ten storeys – and she could only see the roof of the shop. She thought what fun if she could set that shop on fire. So she concentrated hard.

Nothing happened.

It must be too far away. Or perhaps it was fireproof.

There was an empty cigarette packet on the roof near her feet. She tried that. Yes! After a moment it began to smoulder; then it burst into flames.

She tried the shop again. She tried with all her might to set fire to it. She failed; but as she let her eyes wander from the shop, her glance passed over a litter-bin full of paper rubbish, down there on the street.

YES! Quite suddenly it was a ball of flame.

Filled with a sense of power, she pointed her forefingers at two cars coming towards each other along the street below.

She made them swerve!

Almost before she knew what she was trying to do, she brought her fingers together. The cars! They were going to crash head-on! At the very last second, they swerved. But their sides hit, grinding together as they passed. The sound of smashing, of destruction! Diabola loved it.

"YES YES YES!" she shrieked.

Try it on a person!

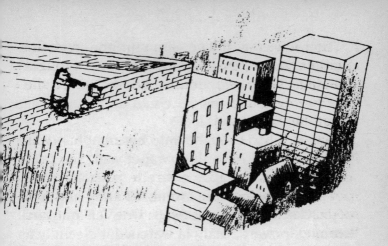

From this height? Could she do it?

She ran to the other side of the roof and pointed at a woman walking along the road. She couldn't see all of her, mostly her head from this angle, but she concentrated on that. The woman stopped walking, started again, stopped, put both hands to her head, bent double – and keeled right over!

People rushed to help her. Diabola jumped up and down with excitement. She aimed at them.

"Pow! Pow! Pow!"

Down they went, one after another, as if Diabola had been shooting them with a high-powered rifle. She only had to stare at them and wish them ill – and *Pow*!

Were they dead? It hardly mattered. If this lot weren't, the next lot would be. When she'd had more practice.

There was a police siren in the distance. Diabola drew back from the low wall and thought, "Now! I can do that. What else?"

If her eyes and fingers could do things, what about her hands and feet?

She sent bad thoughts into her right hand and then banged it onto the parapet wall. She felt it give.

The plaster coating crumbled away and a lot of bricks fell from the wall. One fell outward. Leaning forward, Diabola watched it gleefully as it went down, down, down. A little boy was walking along the path beside the block and Diabola willed him to be right under the brick when it landed.

It nearly worked. He slowed down and stopped, but the brick missed him and smacked the concrete path at his feet, breaking into a thousand fragments. He leapt back, frightened but unharmed.

Next time! Next time!

Diabola was bubbling and hissing and seething with excitement. She thought of Mrs Kirkbright's favourite expression:

"If this is done in the dry wood, what shall be done in the green?"

If Diabola could do this now, what would she be able to do when she had practised? When she was older, stronger, cleverer?

She could hurt anyone, destroy whatever she wanted to, punish anyone she liked, have all the money, all the things, she wanted! Make everyone so afraid of her that they would do anything she told them!

She could make herself safe, and rich, and powerful. She could get all the art materials she wanted. She could draw all the frightening, ugly, violent things in the world. She could invent some nobody had ever thought of! Draw them. Paint them. *And perhaps – perhaps she could make them come true!*

She put her concentration into her feet, and without thinking too much – she was too excited – jumped.

The building rocked. Only slightly. But it rocked!

No! That was stupid. She must be careful. She mustn't endanger herself. She quickly withdrew the power from her feet, and sat down on the wall near the hole she had made. It was a good spot to look down from, to look down and plan.

As soon as she stopped being so excited and began to think properly, she thought of Angela.

She never thought of Angela unless she was there, or unless she needed her.

Why should she need her? She didn't understand this and it infuriated her. She loved no one, of course, but she only hated certain people. She hated her teacher. She hated her mother and father. But Angela she hated worse than anyone in the world. And yet... In some strange way, a way that sucked at Diabola's strength, she depended on her.

She suddenly realised something. Something she had always known but never faced. When Angela was beside her she couldn't always be as bad as she wanted to be.

The nearer Angela was to her, the less free she became to do as she liked. Or – and this was terrifying – if she did, she felt bad about it. Like when Angela had called her good names.

When Angela was touching her – like that first day at school when she had held her hand and led her to the classroom – she couldn't do anything but be good.

She shuddered at this knowledge.

And at this: if Angela were close by, Diabola wouldn't be able to practise.

Suddenly Diabola stiffened.

Angela was coming. She could feel it. Coming close. Coming to fetch her. To – and again, like this morning, an unknown word came to her – to *neutralise* her.

As Angela and her mother climbed the last flight of stairs to the roof, Angela was breathing hard. She was talking and, at the same time, taking deep breaths.

"Mummy, you shouldn't have come. It won't be nice. I'm frightened. She'll be bad. Worse than you've ever seen."

She stopped on the stairs. Her mother, behind her, looked at her. The glow that had radiated from her, in the flat downstairs, had gone away. She just looked like a little girl clinging to the railing, her head down, shivering with fear. How could she be strong enough to do whatever had to be done?

"Don't go up there! Leave her alone!"

Angela's head came up.

"I can't. Don't you see? She's done things already. Big things. I haven't done anything."

"The taxi man—"

Angela shook her head. "Nothing. That's nothing. I didn't know. Till I saw what she could do, I didn't know. Now I feel it... I can change things, make people better, take pain away. And I can undo her things. Only, I need to practise, too."

This thought seemed to put strength into her. She stood straight and turned to face her mother.

"Mummy, what's your name?"

"My name," thought Mrs Cuthbertson-Jones wildly. "What's my name?" She'd almost forgotten it. Her husband, who couldn't pronounce it, had always just called her "dear". Yet names were very important. Calling the twins Angela and Diabola – they shouldn't have done that. They should have called them Jill and Jane. By the time she started calling Diabola Jane, it was too late.

"My name? It's Mwytho. It's a Welsh name. It means—"

"It means 'soft'. You mustn't be soft, Mummy."

She wasn't even surprised at Angela knowing this. Nothing about the twins could surprise their mother any more.

"I'm not," she said. "I used to be. But I'm not now."

"Good."

And Angela stepped level with her mother on the stairs and gave her a hug and a kiss. It was not an ordinary hug and kiss. It was as if she hugged and kissed her for the last time. Yet wonderful, unnameable feelings flowed into Mrs Cuthbertson-Jones through her daughter's arms and lips. Pure goodness, happiness and strength ran through her from top to toe.

"Don't come unless I call you. It's better, Mummy. Trust me."

And Angela ran up the last remaining stairs and pushed open the door to the roof.

21. The Meeting – The Parting

As she came out into the open, Angela looked quickly round.

She saw her sister at once. She was sitting on the parapet beside quite a large broken area in the wall. As Angela came through the door, Diabola turned her head and got up to face her.

She seemed to have grown taller. She had always been a bit taller than Angela, but now, as Angela walked unsteadily towards her, she saw that she had to look up to meet those little glittering green eyes.

"Leave me alone," Diabola said.

"You know I can't," said Angela.

"I'm going to make you. I don't want you around any more."

"You need me."

"I can't need you if you're not here."

"We need each other."

"You'll try to stop me doing what I want."

Angela thought very quickly. Yes. But that meant that Dybo could stop her doing what she wanted, too. The good things she wanted to do.

"I'm stronger than you," Diabola went on. "I can prove it."

"How?"

"Look down there."

Angela walked shakily to the broken wall. Something was making her very afraid. She looked over. Down below she could see several ambulances and a crowd. Some people who looked as if they were dead were being lifted one by one on stretchers into the ambulances.

"Did you do that?"

"Yes. From up here. Just with my eyes."

"Why did you hurt them? You don't know them."

Diabola looked at her as if she were stupid. "So what? I was testing. Watch!"

She stood looking down for only a second. Both the ambulance men who were carrying one of the dead-looking people, fell over.

Without even having to think about it, Angela fixed her eyes and mind on the ambulance men, and at once they began to get up. The person on the stretcher got up, too. It was an old man. He began to dance and caper about. Everyone in the crowd roared. Other people came out of the ambulances and joined in the dance. The next moment, the whole crowd was dancing, shouting and singing. The twins could hear it, ten storeys up.

Angela turned to Diabola.

"You didn't kill them," she said happily. "They're all right. They're fine now."

Diabola looked at her furiously.

"Next time!" she shouted. "Next time, when *you're not here*!"

She pushed past Angela and ran. She ran away from the wall, towards the door to the stairs. Angela thought she'd gone – retreated. So she made a bad mistake.

She turned away from Diabola and looked down again into the street. She wanted to have another look at the first big good thing she'd ever done.

A moment later she sensed Diabola coming back.

She didn't hear Diabola's running feet, though they were right behind her.

Angela knew she was coming because she felt a wave of pure badness against her back. It pushed her just before Diabola's two hands pushed her. A split second's warning.

It gave Angela just time to twist to one side.

She felt her sister's hands grab her blouse.

Then Diabola went over the edge - through the hole she'd made in the wall.

Instinctively, Angela dropped down, behind the wall, beside the hole. As Diabola's weight fell, it pulled Angela against the wall with a jarring thump. Angela grabbed hold of Diabola's hands just as they let go of her blouse.

The weight! The weight pulling at her!

Angela's wrists were tight against the broken edge of the wall. It hurt, it hurt! She nearly let go, but Diabola was dangling, her feet in space. Below her was terrifying emptiness, then – the concrete path. Angela gritted her teeth and held on with all her might.

She felt as if her arms were being pulled out. She couldn't hold on! She tried her powers. But they met another power. The two powers met on the roof-edge.

"Dybo!" she got out between her teeth. "Stop it! I can't hold you!"

Diabola didn't answer. She was pressing the soles of her shoes against the wall, trying to climb up. Angela pulled, scraping her wrists more. Then her wrists came clear of the rough bricks. She was on her knees now, edging back, pulling, pulling Diabola up.

Diabola's face came up slowly over the broken parapet.

Their eyes came level.

Angela saw Diabola's face change.

She saw the terror in it disappear under something stronger.

Angela looked into her twin's eyes. She couldn't even see her fear now. All she could see was hate. All she could feel was Diabola's wish to destroy her.

Angela used every bit of power she had. She wanted – at that moment, she truly wanted – only *not* to let Diabola go. The feeling of

wanting that was so strong she forgot all pain, all fear. She forgot that Diabola had tried to kill her.

She held on. She pulled. But suddenly she felt that Diabola was not letting her pull her up. *Diabola was pulling back.*

In that second Angela knew the awful truth. Diabola was still trying to pull her over. Diabola wanted to destroy Angela more than she wanted to save herself.

Angela let go.

She didn't decide to. It just happened. The sheer shock loosened her grip on Diabola's wrists and they slipped through her hands.

For an instant, Diabola's face hung there, her eyes wide with disbelief, staring into hers. Then she fell.

Down, down, down. Like the brick. Down to the pavement. Screaming all the way. And then –

Splat.

22. Balance

Mrs Cuthbertson-Jones – Mwytho – heard the cry and dashed out onto the roof.

She found Angela lying face down near a hole in the parapet. Her empty hands were reaching out. She was so still, Mwytho thought she was dead.

She rushed to her and gathered her into her arms.

"Angela! Angela! Speak to me, my own, my darling!"

Angela stirred. Her eyes were closed. But she was alive. Her mother picked her up. She carried her down the stairs to their flat.

She'd forgotten Diabola. She'd forgotten the cry she'd heard that had sent shivers of dread through her. All she thought about was Angela, lying unconscious in her arms.

She put her on the bed and covered her. She saw her wrists were scraped. She ran to fetch a wash-cloth to wipe them. She rubbed Angela's hands and patted her cheeks. She kissed her and called her. She didn't know what else to do.

Angela moved and groaned. But she didn't open her eyes.

What could Mwytho do? No phone. No neighbour to help. Nothing!

"Oh, Angela! Help me!" she heard herself say. How foolish! And yet...

Like an answer, came a knock at the door.

She ran through and opened it. Outside stood the vicar.

"Benedict! How did you know to come?"

He didn't answer. His face was white. He came in and took both her hands silently.

"Benedict, what's happened?"

"Poor lady! My poor lady!" was all he could say.

Because he knew.

He had felt a call, he had left the vicarage, found a taxi waiting, driven here, and – as he climbed out of the cab – had happened to look up. Oh, horrible sight!

Mwytho could feel his hands shaking. She could see tears starting to his eyes. And suddenly the echo of that cry came back to her.

"It's Diabola, isn't it?"

He nodded.

"What—"

"Don't ask me, dear lady! Please, don't ask! Just... accept that it's for the best!"

"Dead?" she whispered.

"Yes. Quite, quite dead."

They stared at each other. It was as if neither of them could believe it. For the best?

Mwytho straightened up. He felt her hands grow steady in his.

"For the best," repeated Mwytho, who was no longer soft like her name. "Yes. Now, please, come with me."

She turned and led him through into the bedroom. Angela lay there perfectly still. Her face was pale above the duvet. The vicar bent over her, felt her forehead.

"She's very cold," he said.

"Oh, please!" breathed Mwytho. "She's not going to die – is she? I couldn't bear it!"

"What happened to her?"

"I found her up on the roof."

"On the roof?" The vicar seemed startled.

"Yes."

The vicar straightened and looked down at the figure on the bed. He was thinking deeply.

If this angel-child had been the cause of her sister's death...

Good destroying evil... But in doing so, good would no longer be pure good. If good has to destroy badness, it can't be perfect any more.

The perfect becoming imperfect. Goodness, with a tinge of badness. What would that mean?

He fell on his knees beside the bed and

prayed. What did he pray for? He hardly knew. He prayed for Angela, but not Angela the angelic child. She was no more. He prayed for whatever she would be, now.

"Benedict! Look!"

He looked. Angela had opened her eyes slowly, and was staring up at the ceiling.

The room was very dark. Just a little light coming in from the broken window panes next door. They couldn't see her well.

"Mummy? Has Daddy come home?"

Mwytho caught her breath.

"No, darling. But Benedict's here."

"Daddy will be good enough for us, now."

"What do you mean, darling?"

"Daddy will come. He'll be able to manage, now."

"You mean – now Diabola's – gone?" asked Mwytho in a choking voice.

"Oh, she's not gone."

The vicar's prayer came to a sudden end. His heart jumped and his veins ran icy cold.

Angela's voice sounded much stronger. She sat up and pushed the quilt off.

"Why am I lying in bed in the dark? I'm fine!"

She stood up and walked through into the living-room. The vicar and Mwytho hurried through after her.

"It's cold, Mummy."

Mwytho started. She had never heard that note of complaint in Angela's voice before.

"Yes, darling. I'm sorry. We'll get the glass fixed."

"We don't need to. We won't have to live here when Daddy comes back."

"If he comes—"

"He'll come. And everything will be—" She paused, frowning. "The way it should have been." She turned and walked up to the vicar. "Thank you," she said softly. "Now you can go home." And when he hesitated, she repeated, but with a sharpness he'd never heard, "Go home!"

The vicar was about to look away from her towards her mother, but something about her eyes caught his attention.

He peered closer; then he put his hands on her shoulders and turned her so that she faced the glass panel in the door. He looked at her eyes again. And he gasped.

One was heavenly blue, as it had always been. The other –

The other eye was green.

He looked at it. He saw a glitter in it that told him that Diabola was indeed not gone.

The vicar let go with a deep sigh. He turned to the pretty woman he had, for a brief, insane moment, thought might one day be his wife.

"Dear lady," he said. "She's right. You don't need me now. Balance. Balance has been restored."

"What... what do you mean?"

"Just remember," he said quietly. "There is no such thing in this world as pure good or pure evil. For a little while, there was an exception. But it only proved the rule. Perhaps that's why it was allowed to happen."

He took her hand for a moment, gazed at her, and went out. He felt slightly dizzy and decided a walk down the stairs would be good for him, so he just missed Mr Cuthbertson-Jones coming up in the lift.

A few weeks later, the Cuthbertson-Joneses were living a very different life.

Mr Cuthbertson-Jones, whose conscience was very active, had been only too glad to be found and sent back to his family, though he had a lot of shocks to face when he got there.

How did he feel about Diabola's death? His feelings were so complicated, it's impossible to describe them.

But his feelings about his wife and surviving daughter living in a broken-down, tenth-floor council flat were quite simple. He went straight out and got a job. It wasn't as good as his old one, but it was good enough to rent a nice flat near the school.

He was quite determined to make up for his weakness in running away. He'd realised, while living the miserable life of a homeless person under a bridge, that guilt had brought him to this sad state. He now decided that he'd paid for whatever wrongs he had done (he really hadn't done anything very terrible), and that his best course was to be strong and dependable in future.

He and his wife stopped calling each other "dear". He called her Mwytho (he took the trouble to learn to pronounce it) and she called him Currer. Yes, that was his name. It's from the Latin for "run" but he never lived up to it again.

And they decided not to call Angela Angela any more.

They called her Jill. A lovely, sunny name. An ordinary name.

And Jill? Well, she was now an ordinary normal little girl, with good and bad mixed up in her. Her parents adored her and on the whole she made them happy and proud.

But every now and then she would have flashes of bad temper and outbursts of bad behaviour. And at these times, she developed a squint.

Her blue eye would turn inwards and look at her green eye. The green eye would look back at her blue eye, and grow slitty and glittery. The two eyes would glare at each other across the top of her nose.

Usually the blue eye would get the better of the green eye.

But not always.

Just like the rest of us.